deranged

deranged

three stories

Nora L. Jamieson

Weeping Coyote Press

ISBN 978-0-9962195-0-1

Cover Image: Shreve Stockton, "always the beautiful answer" www.dailycoyote.net. Used by permission.

Acknowledgments

Anne Michaels, *Fugitive Pieces*, McClelland & Stewart, 1998. Mark Tredinnick, *The Land's Wild Music: Encounters with Barry Lopez, Peter Matthiessen, Terry Tempest William, and James Galvin*, Trinity University Press, 2005.

for my ancestors

deranged

Contents

Reckoning

"Revelation is always imminent . . . we will find it in the shape
and body of things in the world."

Mark Tredinnick, *The Land's Wild Music*

Some would say Anna is a toughened woman, strong spirited, raw boned, the lines of grief imprinted on her face. But right now she is perplexed and not a little frightened.

It is midmorning on a warm February day during an odd winter of freeze and thaw. Anna, a tall woman with long white hair, wearing a heavy lumberjack shirt, ragged gloves, jeans, and mud covered old boots, stands by the boulder in the woods north of her small house, the one she can see from her window when she sits by the wood stove.

The breath from her exertions and her fear plumes out around her, an interior heat and life made visible before disappearing into the cold air. Anna leans down to look into the shadowed cave just under the boulder's lip where she's tried to bury the urn of ashes. The earth refuses it. She's been trying to bury it for two days, nestling it into the dirt, covering it, and later on discovering it unearthed, like an old dog bone. But there isn't any dog that she can see. It is a mystery. But one that she is sure has a logical explanation, she tells herself anyway, while aware of the slight and consistent roiling in her gut. She'd come out this morning to check on the stability of things under the boulder, hoping the urn hadn't reappeared and she could forget the whole thing. But no, there it is. She straightens and lays the shovel against the boulder and leans against it to consider things.

Staring at the urn, she thinks how she wants to be done with this, to be done with the carrying of this sorrowful burden that like a bad penny keeps returning. More casually than she feels, she pulls tobacco and papers out of her breast pocket and before she rolls a cigarette she sprinkles a little on the ground in front of her, like her grandfather taught her so many years ago. If this is a mystery, she thinks, I need help. While a disbelieving, if not cynical, part of herself stands aside watching her, she makes an offering, a request that the earth take and redeem what she knows the urn holds. Oh shit, she thinks to herself, redemption again.

She rolls the cigarette, tamps the end. The white paper flares in the shelter of her cupped hands and she draws in a deep stream of smoke, feels her body relax. While she smokes the tobacco she thinks about this wanting of redemption. It is something she ponders often and always has. She drags long on the cigarette, remembering as a child sitting in front of the television, some insipid black and white show she supposes, a TV tray in front of her on which lay a stack of empty booklets filled with black and white squares, each square a tidy home to one S&H Green Stamp, the pages holding thirty or so, she can't remember. Five across, light green with a red S&H, like Christmas.

To her right a small bowl of water sat with a sponge in it. She liked how the stamps ripped predictably and neatly along the perforated line, or when she'd find sheets of stamps given to her mother exactly the right size for the page. This always felt auspicious. She would run it over the damp sponge and paste it in the book which would swell with the moist sheets until it required a rubber band to hold it closed.

She poured over S&H catalogues with lots of stuff they could redeem with their stamps.

The Ladies of the Redemption Center wore white smocks, and rubber tips on their index fingers to riffle through the books, rip out just enough stamps for the little transistor radio or toaster or something she really desired, like a doll, while the conveyor belt rolled on, a great tongue delivering their redemption. But what was redeemed? Is redemption a trade? You give something over and get something back, a better thing than what you gave.

She remembers the large painting that hung over the pulpit and choir in her church. Jesus was kind looking, receiving all the small children, everyone white, like him. She swore that painting breathed as she sat through many dull and juiceless sermons. Christ the Redeemer, he cashes in our sins for us, he is the big S&H Green Stamp, delivering us from evil.

She imagines redemption to be a good clean thing, like new stuff, shiny and unused, that to be redeemed is to feel clean and unsullied in any way. Free. But how does one being do that for another? As a child she figured Christ had an in with god who wipes the slate clean, because if you need redemption then you're not in good standing with god, right? And Christ says to god, Listen, if I give you my whole life for my friends here as long as they promise not to do it again and to believe in your omniscience, then you'll bless them. And god says, Okay.

"Right?" she says to a fat squirrel who watches her closely from its perch atop the elk skull nailed to the goat barn. He assumes the frozen monk posture, paws folded, attentive and waiting, for words or hawk, Anna isn't sure, but it makes her smile.

But then again, she thinks, the Buddhists say that suffering is a result of wanting stuff, even blessings from god, or release from suffering, and can't be healed with more stuff or more wanting but that's not what the Ladies of S&H Redemption would say or the priests either.

Recently she heard a man many thought to be wise say that redemption is making something useful out of suffering, a useful story, or beauty. Making something of value out of it. Anna likes this understanding, but the question nags her, value to whom? She douses the cigarette in the snow, puts the butt in her pocket. For a moment she wonders why she requires redemption, what transgression or failure of heart.

Now she's sixty and each morning she stands and pours corn and seed from her hands onto the boulders north of her house, muttering gratitude, which she has to admit she often doesn't really feel, and prayers for redemption, which she does. Prayers to make something whole and beautiful out of her life. It's not that she feels ungrateful, it's that gratitude is an action, an attending to the sunlight as it warms the stone she leans on, or the cast of shadows on the snow. Crows, having learned her morning ritual, watch her from the trees, and arrogant things that they are, assume the status of gods as they sail down, black and glossy, to receive their due. She finds their tracks in the snowy months, hieroglyphs of a wild, divine entitlement. And then she feels clean inside. Redeemed by crows. It's as good a way as any.

She was never going to be free from wanting, she knew that, but didn't quite understand why, because she'd tried, she'd tried.

The rat-a-tat-tat of a pileated woodpecker catches Anna's attention and she turns to scan the woods for a flash of red and black. She has lived in these woods for thirty years and never tires of the company. She sees him at one of the oldest snags down in the wetlands and reminds herself to put out some suet, an enticement to stay and make more woodpeckers. As she turns back to the boulder, she spontaneously brushes away the snow atop it to reveal veins of pink quartz rivering through the grey stone.

She had a dream that by this very same boulder she'd found long slender fingers of quartz crystal that had once been part of a whole, now sheared off. She laid one piece on the altar of the boulder's back, as if to say, Here is one recovered piece of your broken body. Anna hasn't known what to make of the dream, but suspects it speaks of her broken life, a good life, but not a whole life. Not a cohered life. It seems to her anyway that she has been looking for the pieces forever. Which pieces she doesn't know. But then again, she shrugs, why should her life cohere when the whole world seems mad and fragmented, in bad need of repair.

Crows race by overhead, calling to one another, off on a mission. Anna watches for a while, her face in the weak sun. It comes to her that she's had many dreams of breakage lately, beads scattered and irretrievable.

She stands in her mother's basement apartment. A ragged doorway has been carved in the wall, exposing the dark unfinished basement where there is to be some kind of ritual. Anna is standing in the threshold, wearing a buckskin dress. She is sobbing and suddenly the string holding a crystal necklace around her neck snaps and scatters the beads on the hard floor, some rolling under her mother's flowered loveseat. She can hear them bouncing and pinging in all directions. An old woman, seated on the loveseat, instructs her to gather all the beads, for only then can the old woman do something over them.

Now Anna wonders just what that old woman would do with the scattered beads, even the shards, all the broken and irretrievable things.

Her neighbor, Adam, who cuts holes in the sky, revs his chain saw, startling Anna out of her reverie. The high pitched whine signals that soon the earth will shake. She has watched from her upper window when the huge trees fall, how the astonished light pours down onto the shadowed earth. Later, while walking in the woods, she has felt a kind of shameful gratitude for the sudden circle of light in the dark forest. She knows that after time a new life will generate there, but she can't help but weep when she hears an old tree hit the ground. She sneaks out after he has cut trees on his land and lays offerings on their bleeding stumps.

Adam, never married, has been helpful to Anna ever since her husband died ten years ago, and she is grateful for it, if not his affection which she doesn't fully acknowledge, having decided that there isn't another mate for her. He is a good man, kind. He has, in the past, helped her bury her animals with skill and an open-hearted tenderness in the face of her tears. But he's at it again, she thinks, sighing.

Anna is acutely aware of loss, some would say morbidly so, but she doesn't seem to be able to help herself. Fragments and loss preoccupy her thoughts.

When Anna was a girl, she lay on the grass, staring up at the sky and saying her name over and over until it lost all meaning and sent a thrill and terror through her body as if her name was what gave her what ballast she'd ever had and to lose it was to float up and dissolve into the trees, into the sky. She always felt without

17

substance, without a certain grave density. Where others saw her as a woman who took up space, Anna felt she was not so much invisible as permeable.

She spent the first weeks of life in a crib beside her parents' bed in a small dormered room whose windows overlooked Cedar Street and an old cemetery where the dreams of the dead flew up through the lattice window and fell into her tiny, pink mouth. Later, grown-ups would tell her stories about how she'd clench her fists and teeth, shake and roar with exuberance, eager to be free of the confines of her jumping chair.

The dead wanted life, and Anna was the unwitting carrier of their holy longing. They still had dreams after all. But most of all they wanted to be remembered. All her life she had felt scattered like the broken beads she dreamed, different parts of herself trying to find satisfaction, trying to find peace and home and accomplishment and excitement, a desire to live solitary as a heron and yet nestled within a big family, to be on stage and to hermit. To be all places at the same time. The voices would not be quiet. Sometimes she has felt like a mad woman.

Any wise elder would have seen right away what was happening and protected her, or at the least helped her meet these spirits. The unfortunate circumstance of her birth was that there weren't any wise elders left within a hundred miles. Instead, her parents and their friends, tickled yet alarmed by her wild enthusiasm, laughed and shushed and shaped until the longing retreated into a hollowed out place deep in her breastbone, the place of Shades, where it wore at her and persisted, like a pestle grinding against the soft flesh of her heart until she developed a gristle of tissue scarred and tough. A heart at whose permeable center she carried the grief and longing of many.

Reluctantly, she glances down to where she has tried to bury the urn, hoping that she has imagined the whole thing, but no. She stares at the urn for a while. At a loss, she decides to take a walk in the woods to clear her mind. She goes into the house, grabs her parka and hat and her coffee mug and heads out.

Anna passes through the opening in the old stone wall that separates her wild and overgrown land from the woods beyond. She walks up the hill where she sits on the humped back of a deeply embedded boulder within a grove of white pines overlooking the hills to the south. The wind soughs through the evergreens, speaking of other places, other worlds, other times. She tries to breathe, to take in the starkness of the trees against the bluing sky, to remember that owls are sitting on their eggs now and that all of life is beginning to reach for spring, even in this seeming barrenness. This is one of the places in the world where Anna feels whole, but it is no use, her relentless mind picking up the thread, wandering over scattered beads and shards of quartz. She remembers that there are old stories of those who restring and sing over the bones to reanimate life. A kind of resurrection. Is that what the old woman in the dream intended? That there is a way to gather all the beads and sing them alive and whole?

She thinks of what is in the urn and the impossibility of singing alive what it carries. The boulder was struck and shattered. The string that holds them broke and scattered the beads. And Anna too feels she was struck and broken. She sees herself as a six year-old girl, standing out on the open plain of love, her heart shattered into fragments, the earth riven open and all connection severed by devastating loss and the silence that followed.

Once stricken, did she become afraid of the storm, did she seek shelter, or again throw herself wide open to the surge, taking her chances with life? Like so many say we should? And love? Anna knows what she has done. She has become like coyote, sitting on the margins, the hedgerows, waiting and watching before moving. And then quick, quick, out and back again. Not giving up on life, but not quite putting herself at the center either, lest it be a trap, poisoned meat.

She is not so much cynical as sniffing out the whole story carried on the winds—poison? medicine? She keeps a low profile. Has grown careful in her expressions of love.

On an icy March day in 1954, her father died. After too brief, encoded goodbyes, he was carried away from home on a stretcher to die alone in what Anna imagines as a sterile hospital room in the middle of the night. She had never been told he was dying but she knew in the way a child knows, the dense air full of smoky sorrow, whispered conversations, worse yet, the marrow of their lives sucked clean, the bones hollow.

She was nearly six and the days were a blur of incomprehensible loss amidst the milling bodies of adults dressed in black, ushering her and her brothers to the funeral, ignoring them in its aftermath of cocktails, food, and even laughter. It was the loneliest time of Anna's life, gazing up at those who were left to her, kin who were supposed to have loved and mourned with her, instead holding glasses of golden whiskey and ice, exchanging pleasantries as though the world had not just become a wasteland.

They were telling her, This is how we do it. See?

After her father died, her mother's body went grey and heavy, no comfort. Anna could not eat enough—fried clams, milk shakes, thick and sweet, mother's milk—until she was numb enough to try to live. She rehearsed for the first day of school and the inevitable question, "And your father?" and her impassive reply, "deceased." How odd it must have been for a six year-old to say 'deceased' instead of 'dead.' Or even 'gone' or 'passed away.' And deceased, doesn't that mean not ceased? Resurrected? Undead? In the months after his death she began to have recurring dreams of burying the dead, of witches pulling her into their underworld, of tidal waves. She got fatter and fatter, bloated with grief. Only many years later when she was nearly thirty and finally openly grieving, did she imagine crawling into the coffin with her father and resting in his arms.

In August, six months after Anna's father died, Hurricane Carol slammed into New England, pouring a deluge of rain, swelling the rivers above flood stage and infusing the atmosphere with a kind of wild and terrifying life. Anna's family lived only yards above the river that bellowed and roared, pushed by itself beyond its bounds, a torrent ripping trees, eating dirt, taking everything into itself to feed such an enormous and insatiable hunger. Like grief. She and her brothers stood at the very edge of the sheered off bridge, fatherless, watching muddy flood waters frothing past their feet, moving downriver maddened, carrying everything they knew. Too young to understand why, Anna felt a mysterious relief and kinship with Hurricane Carol, unleashing all the rage and anguish Anna carried alone.

As life moved on, Anna and her family grew more untethered, separated from one another by a particular and unspeakable absence, ghosts lingering with the living.

At sixty, she could hardly remember a time when she *wasn't* the daughter of a man who died a young and tragic death from leukemia. Until Cousin Freda visited. History can rewrite itself like that, with one chance visit. Fifty years after her father's death, Freda told her that the autopsy results revealed that his body was full of DDT. A large woman, short and round, uncannily like Anna's aunt Ruby whom she had loved, Freda leaned forward in her chair, slapped her palm on the table and said, "The damn fool used to hole himself up in that store and spray. They said it was harmless and he believed them." After years of using DDT in the military, fumigating mess tents, her father returned to his own restaurant and used it there.

Suddenly her father's "death after a short illness" became an eerily impersonal, if not quite murderous, death from unnatural causes. Killed. Since Freda's visit, Anna has poured over old ads for DDT in the moldering stacks at the local library, noting the startling shift from cautions in the late 1940s to the mid-50s ads cheerfully giving farmers permission to spray their cow feed with

21

DDT. She even found an old ad with a chorus line of fruit singing "DDT is Good For Me!"

In her less than tender moments, Anna has come to think of DDT as the Dead Daddy Trinity. Dichloro-diphenyl-trichloro cha cha cha. When she was a girl, planes loaded with it flew low over the neighborhood and the crops, letting loose a roar of poisonous dust.

Her mother refused to sign the permission to allow dusting but it didn't matter, majority ruled. Everyone was so frightened about polio. She hears her mother's voice calling them indoors, as if that was any real protection. The river ate the poison and they ate the fish.

Rachel Carson's *Silent Spring* came seven years after her father died of acute leukemia. Anna's mother studied the book and grew increasingly alarmed about its message.

She wonders if her mother had an intuition, confirmed by Carson, that this so-called miracle could kill us. Was that one of the sources of the guilt and rage her mother carried? Did she blame herself?

Anna shivers not so much from cold as from her speculations. The sun is streaming down through the pines now, the broken light making little pools of warmth on the softening snow. She drinks from her mug, noticing around her a dark vein etched under the snow's surface. She imagines herself a vole, traveling highways under the predator free peace of deep snow. She wonders at the life lived below a cold and pristine surface.

Because Anna wasn't there and they never spoke of it, she tries to imagine the state of mind and the day that would move her mother to commit such an act of violence. She imagines it was a day in winter when the wood stove was lit, probably a Sunday. Her mother may have lain in bed throughout the morning listening to evangelical sermons on the radio. Perhaps feeling uplifted and hopeful, she got up, showered, dressed, and made a sandwich for lunch along with a whiskey to celebrate all the possibilities. She sat at the small dining table, looking out at the trees as she ate something she loved, followed by the parsed out chocolate she always kept in the cupboard. Perhaps she was in a kind of reverie, feeling and loving the magnificence of the world, the trees against the light, the woodpecker at the suet. Anna knew this about her mother, those jewels in her mother's medicine, her capacity for wonder and reverence. And then, at the peak of the swell, perhaps she turned, with a kind of breathless anticipation toward the rest of the day, finding herself carried down the long corridor of a lonely afternoon looming out ahead of her. Despair blossomed in her heart.

Maybe she rose then, poured another whisky, and sat at the old Royal typewriter, a permanent guest at the place across from her at the table. The keys clickety-clack, like skeletons in the windy void. What might she have written on that day? Perhaps she is Madame DeFarge, knitting in words the whole story of her fury. Or Demeter, writing lamentations of her loss.

As time passes, her mother pours out all the words that can outrun despair, some of them beautiful, Anna is sure, and an unbearable silence fills the space. She pauses to gaze out the window, not failing to notice the lowering sun and the color of the sky. Never failing to notice.

Perhaps she rises to stand at the sink, her gnarled hands moving over the porcelain with an old dishcloth, alternately cleaning up a bit and looking through the window. Waiting.

Late afternoon and maybe another whiskey to make the work and loneliness lighter, the time pass faster. She leans against the sink, staring into the near dusk. She notices how the winter sun backlights the empty clothesline, casting shadows out across the snow, stark and beautiful, reaching to the edge of her window. She wishes she had someone to tell about this, but there is no one. No one who would understand. Grief and bitterness seize her. Why am I alone, she asks as she stands, crying, until, numbed by the familiar oppression of restraint, she straightens, turns away from the sink into the room. She thinks of her daughter, Anna, longs for her, wonders where she is, and her eyes fall on the photo albums there on the bookcase, remembering how Anna has, for the past year, retrieved them from the shelf at each and every visit, full of questions about the people there. Again and again. Maybe life is there.

Anna winces as she remembers these times as good between them, close, speaking of things that matter. But her mother told her very little.

There are two albums and a box. The box contains photos from her mother's generation, people Anna has never met or heard of. The albums are more personal to Anna—baby pictures, her mother and father. There is a red album and a green one, large with black pages, each photo inserted into corner tabs and labeled in her mother's handwriting with white ink.

Some photos are yellowing, blotting out the image. A child, arm cheerfully raised in a gesture of waving, his hand disappearing into a yellow blob moving across the image, an alchemical mystery that would soon consume him completely, the way Anna's ancestors seemed to disappear into a fog of forgetting.

Some photographs are memorable. The one of her Aunt Elsie in her checkered red and black hunting jacket, rifle held under her arm, smiling into the camera. Her mother as a child wearing a large bow pinned into her long curly hair, perched on a stone wall alongside her mother and father and brother, who wore a jaunty cap, broadleaf tobacco growing around them. Most of her mother's people were farmers. Anna, who cannot grow a thing, credits them for her affinity for the land, place, rain, sky.

Anna wonders if her mother resented her interest in the past. These were her people after all, not Anna's, *her story*, not Anna's. Could that explain why she sorted out the few baby pictures for Anna and her brothers, and then destroyed the rest?

Or perhaps it had been a really good day, a good day to begin anew a life that had seemed over. A good day to make a clean slate like a blanket of new fallen snow. Was this her mother's attempt at redemption—a way to feel clean, to begin again by incinerating memory? There is no way for Anna to know, but her heart tells her that her mother was purging pain, her heart poisoned by grief, fabricating all the reasons she should burn the past. Or perhaps both.

In any case, the past is ashes. Except Anna knows now that it is not. Even if all the photos are gone, she has experienced how the past lives in the tissues and empty spaces, in the longing and despair, in the stories told and not told, in the shape of a nose or the calling of a soul. It lives on, neither grieved nor understood, the future carrying the past like DNA.

The yellowing images of people whose stories she'd never known, wouldn't know, but who were her blood, remain. Anna recalls a photo of her father standing with her aunt and uncle who lived in an apartment above his store. With a start she realizes that all three died within three years of each other. Dead from cancer, all three. Was it the DDT?

As a young woman, Anna had poured over those photos, looking, searching for something to anchor her. Family.

She tried to read these photographs like braille, running her eyes over the pictures again and again, seeking some recognition, some missing piece that would help her to feel whole. Someone cared enough to want to keep the youthful aspirations and longings and pain recorded here. Why couldn't she read them?

CHILLED, ANNA STANDS and begins to walk with a kind of urgency through the snow, noting the tracks of deer, fox, coyote, and white mice as she ponders that day.

Her mother's face looms, licked by the dancing flames, an oscillating collage of revenge, regret, fury, and grief as she reckons with each image and memory and tosses them into the fire, flames growing hotter with each spirit.

Is the urn of ashes that has turned up nearly thirty years later evidence of remorse? Perhaps her mother's anger with life cooled as the fire raged. Perhaps it was then that she realized what the pictures meant to Anna. If so, Anna imagines the self-recrimination the next day as her mother carefully gathered and poured the ashes into the ginger jar, storing it away for after her death.

She knows the jar well—an heirloom from her grandmother, perhaps lovingly carried on some ship heading for America, the beauty of its deep indigo blue always a comfort to Anna who, as a small child, would secret the small found bones of animals in its dark interior. It seems fitting that it has become an urn.

A memory of going to church with her mother washes over her, the two of them leaving the warmth of the dusk lit yellow kitchen, walking hand in hand in the biting February air to the small church, returning with ashes crossed on their foreheads as they made their way home down Main Street, Anna filled with a sense of mystery, the possibility of spring in the air.

Her mother never told her about the urn, even on that inevitable day when Anna went in search of the photos. Her mother's face was placid as she turned to her, "I burned them." Anna sat, stunned and flattened, unable to comprehend what felt like such an act of pure hatred, her heart withered. But now she wonders, who did her mother hate?

Her thoughts turn toward the urn that will not be buried.

"And what am I supposed to do with them now?" She asks of her long dead mother, her words evaporating into the dry winter air. "Am I to sing over these fucking ashes?"

Anna is descended from an embittered female lineage. Women who traveled across oceans in a ruthless migration, running from poverty, leaving the land they loved and called home, leaving families never to see them again. Women descended from those accused and damned as witches, tortured and burned, witnessed by their daughters who would one day have daughters of their own. To whom they would impart fear and repression and self-hatred along with mother's milk. Mothers who would be confused by feelings of love and hatred for their children and wonder at the now invisible root of such evil. A poisonous brew erased from memory, simmered and reduced to a burnt ash of compressed hatred, igniting and flaming out of control. And existing alongside love.

Her ancestors, women torn. Better to forget. Better to burn the pictures.

Anna winces, suspecting that her passionate love for the past, her need for family, for roots, was the match to her mother's bitter harvest, illuminating a life too painful to rekindle.

And her own life? Unable to forgive her mother, she has rocked this lump of coal, this bit of ash, this twisted grief inside for so long that she fears that, unlike the Buddhist Saints who leave relics of hope and inspiration, hers will be a bitter and cursed legacy. Even as her heart begins to soften, her mother's cold declaration, "I burned them," rises up, igniting her rage like dry tinder.

She stalks out of the woods, her finger jabbing the air, and yelling aloud to the surrounding trees, "If forgiveness is part of redemption, I am doomed. So fuck it." She grabs the shovel and furiously digs a deeper hole, shoves the urn in with her foot, kicks dirt and snow over it, grabs the shovel and marches back toward the house.

The urn flies out and hits her on the back with a muffled thud, shoving her to her knees. Always choosing rage over fear, Anna springs up, slowly turns around, looking to curse the force, the being, the spirit, the evil, that will not let her be done with this.

Nothing. And still nothing. A bell jar settles down around Anna, engulfing her in a preternatural silence. No chitter or call or wind whistle, no thaw drip. She stands, quiet, wondering just where she is, waiting. Someplace not here, she thinks, sending a message of fear racing through her. She hunches over, hands on her knees, trying to breathe while her body twitches and thrums with adrenaline. Sobbing, she sucks in lungsful of cold air. I'm dying, no I've died, runs through her mind, escalating her panic.

Sounding to her own ears like a wild thing, trapped and afraid, she stops.

Bird call, squirrel, wind, drip. Here.

It is something she has known how to do for a long time, as long as she can remember. She stands, wipes her face, looks around.

Her four penned goats watch her suspiciously, ears twitching with alarm. Something is wrong with the woman today. In seeing them, she is embarrassed. "I'm one of those scattered beads," she says to their wary faces. They pull their necks back and lower their heads, looking even more doubtful as to her sanity. Something about this brings her to her senses. She chuckles. "I've got to get a grip on myself." She talks in the soothing goat voice they recognize, and seeing that the woman is returning to herself, the goats ease and shake themselves loose from the tense moment. Taking courage from their animal presence, their just what is, she collects the nerve to look at the urn, knowing she has to gather it up, face whatever is happening here.

She bends down to retrieve it and what spilled ashes she can, and there, on the crusty snow, the dark, intense eyes of her father look up at her. The photograph is yellow and singed by fire that oddly stopped short of his eyes. Only his tender, earnest gaze remains, penetrating into Anna, taking her breath away. She reaches her old rough hand down to retrieve an image she's never seen, captured nearly sixty years ago, long before she was born.

It must have been her mother's private photograph of her husband, not her children's father, but *her husband*. Her mother had tried to burn it too, this precious memory, her beloved. Anna weeps because she truly knows that burning the photos was not purely a personal act of retaliation against her, but also one of desperation, an attempt to excise a past that Anna insisted on keeping alive.

28

Once again an object of goat curiosity, she sits heavily on the steps of the front porch, her head in her hands, tears pooling and freezing on the stone step like tiny Herkimer diamonds.

Soft goat bleats arouse her. Wiping her eyes, she notices the sun has moved far southwest and she is cold, chilled to the bone. Feeling heavy, she pushes herself off the step and moves to feed the goats their beloved grain and barn them in for the night. She stands to watch them gather around the black bucket, nudging each other aside, competing for the sweetness. Before she closes the door, she lets them nibble at her fingers, checking for any sweet residue. A soft, bristly ritual that she loves. Gathering the urn with the salvaged ashes, she goes into the house and puts a couple of logs on the fire and a low heat under the soup she made the night before.

She pours herself a whiskey and while the soup heats she sits in front of the fire, realizing how exhausted yet strangely alert she is. She removes her father's picture from the breast pocket of her shirt, sips the whiskey as evening surrounds her. A pink and purple shawl of dusk shoulders the hills to the west, settling down for an early darkness. The shadows sift down through the lacework of oaks and black birches, quaking aspens and laurel, sheltering owl and flying squirrel, racoon and opossum, finally lying over the shallow winter refuge of the box turtle whose dreams will rise up through Anna's window when she slumbers under the feathers of geese. Oh, how good, she thinks, to slow and descend each winter in a long contemplative sleep. To not chafe against destiny and history, or the dark.

Accompanied by a low hum of running commentary on the day's events, she eats her soup, washes up and gets into bed, putting the urn and her father's picture on the bedside table. Barred owls call outside her window, *who cooks for you, who cooks for youuuu?* No one, she thinks.

When she is worried, it comforts her to remember all the unseen life carrying on around her, all the life in the trees, owls

29

sitting on their eggs, turkeys roosting for the night, the life on the ground, deer bedding down in the trees, raccoons and bears denned away, garter snakes in their ancestral underground dens, huddled for warmth.

Like the box turtle, Anna imagines that she can descend into the long dark. Like a child's game she plans what she will take on this journey. I'll take this skin, these bones, laid bare, spare. I'll take a bag of nails to hammer the door closed from the inside, sealing myself into winter's womb, away from reaching hands, shoulds and coulds, oughts, and have-tos. Dishes pile in the sink, spiders spin in corners and make silver webs of sun and moon. While I, in my root cellar, with the smells of my own body, my own bones, my own pen and paper, gestate in an egg of dirt and roots and time. All the time wasted, dissipated, dissolved into the frozen fertile soil of winter.

She falls asleep as the Full Moon rises over the cabin in the deep cold night, the same moon the Cheyenne people call the Bony February moon because it is the time when the people gnawed on bones to feed their increasing hunger. Anna is gnawing too, but it is on the bone of memory. Her mind scratches and scurries like a mouse in the wood pile, looking, looking for refuge and at the same time her heart thrills to the call of the coyote pack just over the hill, a few of whom she knows well. Near morning she drifts into deeper sleep and dreams.

It is night. She is standing on the beach in a small protected cove by the sea. An old native woman sits by a fire at the water's edge while others launch out to sea in little boats. A man sets out into a dark swell while Anna drums for him. The wild haired old woman turns toward Anna who stands some distance from the fire. "Everyone here drums for themselves," the old woman tells her. Thinking this an instruction, a reprimand, Anna stops drumming. Confused, she waits.

The old woman, her leathery face burnished by firelight, leans toward her and asks, "What are you doing here, what is your story?" Startled, Anna hesitates, wondering, then replies, "I carry my father's death in my basket."

The old woman begins to sob, rivulets of tears wash down her deeply lined face which looms toward Anna, closing the distance between them, "Your unacknowledged grief is terrible."

Anna sits bolt upright in the bed. The moon infuses the room with an insistent light, the air thrums with want, her blood rushes, her head whooshes like a flash flood through dry canyon, sounding an alarm. *Run! Run!* The urn is tipped over on the bedside table, the ashes spilled and smoothed into a tablet by an unseen hand. The photograph of her father lays atop the ashes, his eyes gazing out from another time, arcing a distance she has tried to traverse her whole life. Inscribed in the ashes, next to his picture, is a circle.

"Okay, I'm scared," she says to the empty room. She sits frozen for what seems a long time, turns on the beside lamp, and looks into the pulsating shadows, wondering how she will defend herself if there is an intruder. She remembers the baseball bat under her bed, a parting gift from an old friend. Knowing there isn't an intruder, but knowing someone is after her, she talks to herself, "It's okay, it's okay, it's okay."

It is not that she is a stranger to the uncanny. She has, no matter what befalls her, maintained an openness to possibility, the kind of openness that arises from perceiving the world as a confounding mystery. She is always slightly breathless to see what will reveal itself. A woman who holds her own council, she pays attention, owing both her reticence and her curiosity to her mother's lineage, women who carried mystery, a vestige of the old ways, an appreciation of beauty, a spark that couldn't be extinguished, though nearly. Those women understood an older, more essential order than the current world Anna finds herself in. She wonders if that is where she is now, another order.

She sits hunched in the bed, her arms around her knees, not daring to relax, trying to work it out. She can't stand these koans that wring her mind into riddles of confusion. Yet she feels if she can find what connects yesterday to the dream, something will be revealed.

31

Two fires, two old women, one burning a past that is now mysteriously returned, the other lamenting a grief not acknowledged. And the boat and the man. And the drum.

When Anna sees it, her heart swells like the dark waters carrying the man into the night. It is her father launching out into the sea, and she has been drumming for him her whole life. Drumming to keep him alive and near.

Gripped between the rough hands of some washerwoman god, Anna's heart wrings and twists in on itself, water pouring from her in a torrent like the flooded river of her childhood. Wailing, she grabs for trees, rocks, anything that might anchor her, keep her from drowning in the past. But it is no use. There are no handholds, nothing can stanch the sorrow.

The shadows, gathered in witness, are slowly dispelled by the dawn light fingering up through the trees as she lies spent. She feels both swollen and emptied, bleary and clear, frightened and relieved, and wonders at this sudden, almost violent wrenching of her heart and the events of the past two days.

The goats, as always, bring her back.

She hears them stirring and blatting and knows she must get up and go to them. Yet she feels unable to move and lays in the bed, wondering what time it is, just what realm she is in.

She worked her first spell when he died. The black large-bottomed rocker moved in rhythm to her incantation, "I love you, daddy, I love you, daddy, I love you, daddy, I love you, daddy." A child leading him across the threshold to the other side, keeping the connection to him alive, making sure he knew he was loved. Making sure he didn't fly off into the blackness of space to circle for eternity. An incantation to hold him close as he passed over.

But the old woman tells her that every person here drums for themselves. Where is 'here' exactly? Is she telling me to stop drumming for him? Anna feels a searing in her chest just thinking of it. What is the difference between a grief acknowledged and not? Unacknowledged losses. Are there things that have been lost that she doesn't even realize are gone? Hasn't she suffered enough? Might there be a map in the heart for what has been lost? The disappeared, the disappearing? For old forests, for wolf, for fathers? Her mind skitters off the hard surfaces of her questions.

Your unacknowledged grief is terrible. Perhaps she means in the old way—awesome, putting terror in the heart. Terrible. Anna is visited by visions of women rending their clothing, their hair, wailing for those they will never see again. She remembers an old newspaper photograph of a weeping woman holding the smiling skull of her son retrieved from a mass grave. Found.

She knows in her bones that she carries grief every day of her life, that the old woman knows this too, so what does she mean, *unacknowledged?*

This old woman's burnished face is familiar. She is the one with the beads. That old woman has something to do with all of this, Anna is sure.

The goats are yelling and kicking now and she turns to look out the window. The blue light of early morning reveals the outlines of trees and the boulders down below. Reluctantly, she puts her feet on the cold floor, stands and goes to the window, intuiting a presence. And there, in the distance, is a hawk, hardly distinguishable from the snow, except for the soft white of its underwing as it lofts from the ground into a slender black birch. Through the window she hears a squirrel whine a warning, then hush. A hard way to make a living, she thinks as she pulls on her sweater, overalls, and thick socks. Her days always start this way, and glad for the predictability of it this morning, she descends the stairs to lay the fire. But first the goats, who nearly burst out of the barn with frustration. "That's a bit how I feel," she tells them. Water, feed, scratches, and some conversation and she's back in the house.

Now the fire. As she crumples paper, she takes up the thread.

Ever since he died she has attended more to what is invisible than seen. She is waiting for the moment of his return. The moment of the second coming. Where did he go? Into what ether did he disappear? She recalls a day a few weeks after her father died. She was standing at the edge of the sandlot next to her house, looking out over what seemed like a desert, across to where her new neighbor Karen stood on bare skinny legs. "My father says your father will be in purgatory forever because he's not Catholic," Karen yelled across the distance. Her words conveyed visions of Anna's father forever circling in a profound state of loneliness. She received the cruel blow from a distance, both stunned and barely present, her spirit slipping out at the first whiff of danger. "My father isn't dead," she said, "he has returned. He is in the house reading the paper." For one comforting moment, she believed it.

She looks down at her hands covered with black ink, holding a half twisted newspaper, and she shakes herself like her old dog used to after a good standoff with some wild danger.

She lays the wood, kindling, small split logs, large old pieces.

She's been waiting her whole life for the absence to emerge into presence. She waits for it in the woods, in dreams, in her thoughts. She waits for the coyotes to emerge from the night through their song, or the scream of the fox, the call of the barred owl. It proves something to her. It proves emergence, it proves revelation, it proves that the world is enfolded in on itself and if one is blessed by fate, one is there at these moments of revelation, disappearance, and emergence. I was here, now I am gone. But I was here, yes. I am here. You simply cannot see me. Keep watching and waiting. I am here, yes. I am. They are. He is.

She strikes the match and lights the newspaper, leaving the woodstove door ajar to feed the fire. She stands to wait for the flames to catch full and strong, leans against the window where her breath makes fog on the pane as she stares into the woods at no particular thing. She calls it the gateway, a natural opening between the end of an old rock wall and a stand of arching birches several feet away. She thinks of the many animals she has seen use this passageway, either entering or leaving the woods surrounding the house.

Putting her forehead against the cold glass, she closes her eyes. The icy window is bracing and, she hopes, clarifying. She stands there for several minutes.

"Who is that old woman and what is she telling me?" she said to the empty room. She can see her clearly, feels relieved looking into the round and craggy face. The words 'unacknowledged grief' float through her mind like a mantra, their meaning no more clear.

She raises her head to look out the window just in time to see something swaying, stumbling into the gateway.

She watches the slow crumble of joints, as if disassembled by pulling the connecting thread from the long and graceful legs, first front, then back, then spine, then head, and finally from the heart.

She stands holding her breath, frozen in a ripping imperative to run toward and to run from. "Poison." The voice reaches into her numb witnessing. "Poison," says the old woman. "Again."

Anna runs now, shoving her feet into her boots before bolting out into the frigid air. She nearly flies over the snow into the clearing, stopping suddenly to kneel some distance from the body. Her breath explodes in white clouds. She looks hard at the body. No breath joins hers. She can feel the life so newly lifted as she crawls a bit closer, her fear and her love wrestling inside her. She stops and sits and waits. She slows her breathing, knowing there is only time now. Her inclination is to pray, but for what?

She moves closer and lays her hand on the coyote's winter ruff. She recognizes her, they've met before not far from here on many of Anna's walks in the nearby woods. She thanks the coyote for her beauty and presence. She weeps, remembering how she has watched the coyote for years, herself gaining courage from her ability to survive. Until now. She must have been particularly hungry to let down her guard in this way. To eat poison.

Anna wants to lay her body down on the body of the dead coyote but she doesn't want to burden this leaving spirit as if the coyote is Christ on the cross dying for our sins, again. Is she seeking the old redemption even at this hour? She's disgusted with herself. Coyote is not her Christ or scapegoat. She is Coyote.

Gathering the coyote in her arms, she stumbles to her feet and carries her back to the cabin. Warm and soft, the lifeless body drapes across her open arms, the yellow foamy spittle on her muzzle the only indication of the poison that killed her. She lays her under a thick bramble of mountain laurel where she is somewhat sheltered, kneels there for a while to numbly sprinkle tobacco on her body with a prayer, and goes into the house to tend the fire. She's not sure what else to do.

She selects a large piece of split oak and when it proves too big for the stove, she uses a poker to jam it into the box, jabbing the log with increasing violence until anger and futility overtake her. Swearing, she grabs the log with tongs, flings open the front door and throws the smoldering wood out into the snow, slamming the door on its hissing.

She paces the room from window to window, yelling into the emptiness, "Where is the fucking redemption now? Huh? Beauty my ass. If I could even *make* beauty out of this ugliness, what the hell would be redeemed? Who? Poison is poison and dead is fucking dead. And suffering is suffering."

She stops and looks out the window, staring at the coyote's corpse under the laurel. Acid rises in her throat, images of the coyote choking and writhing bring Anna to her knees, as though her strings, too, were cut. She is crazed with grief and rage. Remembering the aftermath of the dream just hours before, she refuses to be overcome again. She gets to her feet and moves into the kitchen where she hunches over the sink and gulps cold water from the tap, as if she were crouched at the stream down below, muzzle in the cold water, trying to slake a killer thirst. Who is she, woman or coyote? The pain is *that* close. She leans against the sink for a while, breathing deeply, getting her bearings.

Tea will help.

The thought is so ludicrous that she laughs bitterly. "So fucking civilized." Yet she pulls the old blue and crazed teapot off the shelf and fills it with water. She puts the pot on the wood stove and while waiting for the water to boil she sits in the rocker to gather herself and to think. She rocks and tries to puzzle it out. And rocks. The way she used to after her father died.

Her eyes settle on the coyote who lies undisturbed as the wind riffles her fur. "What am I going to do? What is there to do?"

She considers the old woman's words about unacknowledged grief and her own inability to help the coyote and how bitterly angry and hopeless she feels in the face of its suffering. And the violence of her rage.

Who would do that? she wants to know and then, oh, and a sinking awareness that she would and did.

Many years ago she hired an exterminator to kill the mice in her house. For months she had lived with mice poop in the bread drawer, frayed electrical cords, and sleepless nights while they conducted their busy lives above her head. She opened drawers cautiously, never knowing who might make a fast exit or if she'd find the pink bodies of mouse babies curled into tufts of insulation. She'd convinced herself that they belonged outdoors or, at the least, outside her house. Property rights. But there was also her primordial dread of dying in a fire ignited by deadly arcs of chewed wires inside her walls. At the time, she felt scared and overrun and at the end of her wits. So she did it, hiring the man who put ominous black boxes full of tasty poison under stairwells, along mice corridors where they would eat and then be driven by devastating thirst to seek water outside. That was the terrible plan. But it didn't work, and for months Anna lived with the stench of rotting mouse bodies and stumbled upon their small bloated corpses and the desiccated bodies of pups.

That her fear led to a deep frustration, yes, even rage, and a declaration of war against the small big-eyed bodies of mice, deeply shames her now.

She gets up to put another log on the fire, watches as the wind, whistling through the woods, scoots columns of powdery snow ahead of itself, looking for all the world like flying ghosts. Just outside the line of her vision, a wisp of understanding appears briefly, peripherally, the way the spirits are said to do. She sits down to puzzle it out. Something about fear, human fear, she waits as it coalesces like mist into fog, fear alchemizing into as volatile and poisonous a concoction as DDT and whatever killed the coyote. There are three poisons here, she realizes.

"But only one can be made into medicine," adds the old woman.

Anna puts the notice in the paper the next day.

Eastern Grey Coyote died on February 10th from an acute illness after suffering excruciating convulsions and suffocation. Cause of death: poison. Eastern Grey Coyote will be remembered for her exemplary mothering, having raised several litters in the woods surrounding Mountain Road, and for her haunting songs and keen survival skills. Having been displaced numerous times from her home habitat, she developed the capacity to make do without assistance. She was an avid hunter of small rodents, favoring field mice and chipmunks, but would eat carrion when need be. She displayed strength of character, curiosity and a playful humor even in the face of intense hatred. She will be dearly missed by those she leaves behind, her family pack and Anna Holmes of Mountain Road who is holding calling hours on February 12th from 9p.m. to midnight. All those who grieve the loss of Coyote are welcome to attend.

Her phone began to ring off the hook as they say. Her brother figured she'd finally gone around the bend and her neighbors kept her on the phone arguing about the threat of coyotes and the benefits of poison, even though they also acknowledged the dangers.

Inevitably people pulled the goat card. She ought to know better, she keeps goats after all. Anna knows. Coyote has more than once come sniffing around the goats and it pains her to think of them dying in that way. But she cannot seem to choose. Her indecision, she's often feared, is a failure of courage. It is a war of sorts, isn't it after all? Can't the killing be defended if committed in the name of defending your property, your own kin? Doesn't she love the goats enough, for god's sake, to defend them? But she loves them both. That is the problem. Love.

The day of the funeral rises clear and sunny. Anna asks Adam to dig a shallow hole, which he does, keeping his own counsel the whole time. He knows she isn't nuts, but he thinks she is overly soft. He listens to her instructions without comment—she doesn't want it so deep that the coyote can't go back to earth, or so shallow that hungry predators will try to dig her up for a meal. She had considered bringing her to the woods for just that reason, but the coyote was poisoned and a danger to the hungry.

At nine o'clock, Anna lights the fire she built earlier in the day and sits down to wait. The black dome of sky arcs down and cups the earth within its dark radiance as the fire casts Anna in a coppery sheen. The coyote lies on the boulder not far from the fire. A breeze fingers her ruff while the firelight flickers off her coat enlivening her even though she is completely frozen, her eyes foggy with absence. She is surrounded by evergreens and a large candle sits on the ground below her. A bowl of tobacco and a bowl of corn meal from Anna's garden sit on the boulder as well. Anna's breath catches when she notices that something has chewed away at the coyote's muzzle, nature's mercy in such a hard winter.

Headlights strobe through the woods from the road winding up to the cabin. The sound of car doors shutting carries in the clear air, as does the squeaking snow of mourners wordlessly following the path to sit by the fire. Anna nods to each as they arrive within the light, three young women, one she recognizes from the local coffee shop with her purple hair, nose rings, and tribal tattoos. She has brought a couple of friends, Anna supposes, and four women Anna's age she has seen at community events. And then there is an old woman who is a stranger to her. "Emma," she introduces herself, thrusting her hand out in greeting, a short and round woman whose silver hair sticks up in spikes around a face that could only be described as puckish. Anna can't decide whether her hairdo is intentional, the result of neglect, or electrical. Leaning in closer, she can see just how wrinkled the woman is, but as it is with puckish people, Anna finds, it's hard to get a bead on just how old they are. They kind of oscillate.

The women sit, their eyes coming to rest on the coyote, then the fire, then Anna, then back to the coyote. What had been lines in the paper, what had been an idea, whatever motivations had brought them here, all fall away in the fact of the coyote's body, the truth of her torturous death that at least one woman had wanted to acknowledge, even in the face of ridicule. They sit for several minutes as in them rises the knowledge that they, too, are now one of those women.

Anna throws more logs on the fire.

Unable to tolerate any more silence, the young woman from the coffee shop speaks first and urgently, the firelight glinting off her purple hair and the dance of her hands as she punctuates her demand that we must learn to live differently with the wild.

Another speaks with fondness, remembering this coyote hunting at the perimeter of her large yard and how she looked for her each morning and dusk. Some loved her up close, others from a distance. They stare at the fire, the pine logs snap and pop flinging sparks into the night.

And then, from another woman, a confession.

"I killed her."

Stunned, they turn to the woman and wait.

"It was from my farm, I'm sure. I deliberately put the poison out after finding one of the sheep dead." She speaks through a scrim of tears, "I put the flock out to get some sun on a warmish day, then found my dear old ewe dead with a typical kill pattern of the coyote. They attack from behind you know, right into the guts. I mean, can you imagine the pain?"

"No, they don't," snaps Anna. "That's probably dogs. Coyotes usually puncture the neck. It's a quick kill." She is really angry now.

The woman falters, sees Anna's outrage. "I didn't know that." They wait.

"So I put poison into her and left it there. I was so angry and so broken hearted. The coyote came back to feed some more, then haul away and cache the rest as I knew it would." She went on to tell them that she'd got the stuff, called 1080, from her brother in Wyoming the last time she visited. It was big out there. When she'd checked the next day, more of the sheep was gone, but not much and she guessed what happened. There was some relief in the vengeance, she admitted.

"But now I'm heartsick. When I saw the paper, at first I felt angry about your placing that outrageous obituary. After all, obituaries are for people, not animals, and this coyote was threatening my livelihood. I called other friends who farm and they sympathized with me. But when I went to bed last night, I had a dream." She paused for several breaths. "And then something turned over inside me."

And it is now that Anna remembers her, from their work around violence against women. And that was years ago. Anna always sensed that her own quiet intensity made the woman uncomfortable, thinking Anna too fierce. Anna sits, waiting, her anger a force field demanding to be reckoned with. She heard a story about this woman years ago. That a black bear, spring hungry, had entered her sheep pen in the night and was attacking one of her sheep. Her husband had recently died, Anna remembers, and she had called a neighbor woman to come and help. They entered

41

the sheep pen armed and dangerous with a rolled up newspaper and a broom. They beat that bear off the sheep. The bear had the good sense to leave and the sheep made it through with some scratches.

"I dreamed that a pack of coyotes was sniffing around me and a couple of friends. It was dusk and we were standing on the edge of the field and they began to howl. I was frightened. I said to my friend, "They sound close by," and she said, "They are close by," and then they were among us, milling around, friendly. My husband leaned down to greet one of them and I warned him to be careful, they being wild, after all. Then this amazing thing happened. I stood frozen, with my hands behind my back, and felt the soft muzzle of a coyote sniffing my hands and then it turned into a young boy who slipped his hand into mine. He was about ten years old and dark skinned. He was a gypsy boy. He was clearly my boy in the dream, not my son, but deeply related to me. I loved him. I knew somehow he'd been captured and I asked if they were educating him. He said no.

"And now I don't know . . . but I'm here because I couldn't stay away and because I did it. I killed her. Because I could and I was aggrieved about my sheep. And scared. And guilty. I guess it was a kind of revenge or way to make the grief and even guilt bearable, that I hadn't protected my ewe. And now I can't undo it. Two dead, for what?

"But then between the obituary and the dream, I had to admit that the coyote had a family and that we were sharing the land. Even though I wasn't even born when my great grandparents farmed this land, I realize that continuing to take the space away from the coyote is a way of killing it as surely as it killed my sheep."

They sit in silence for a long time. To have such a familiar face on the coyote's killer is sobering. It's so much easier to be furious with an anonymous murderer, Anna thinks. But this killer sits at their funeral fire, the coyote's body gleaming on the boulder, stiff with the cold but still somehow sentient and alive. And the dream. And her remorse.

"I see now, though, that when coyote kills, it's bloody and obvious and necessary and immediate. But our killing of coyote is a slow death by exhaustion, starvation, displacement and cars."

"And poison," says Anna.

"Yes, and poison."

Emma speaks now.

"I have been told, or maybe I read it somewhere, doesn't matter, that there was a time when coyotes changed into people and people into coyotes, and deer and frog and fish and hawk. It was the responsibility of these shape-shifters, that's what they called them, to keep good relations based on deep empathy with all of creation. And it wasn't just people, no, it went all round. There were those who were rabbit-coyote, coyote-rabbit so the rabbit would know how hard the coyote worked and the coyote might know the terror and generosity of the rabbit. So nothing could become too removed from creation and all beings could keep the good ways and the heart clear." She pauses to gather her breath.

Tolerant, as so often people are with old ladies, not fully trusting their authority, they all sit politely fixed on Emma, who looks back at them with a wry innocence. "I see you're looking a bit doubtful. Shall I continue?"

The women murmur encouragement and Emma continues, "So if I might venture an opinion here, I think the boy in your dream is a shape-shifter. It's not the people who captured him who will educate him. They will surely kill him. He, having been coyote, has been educated by coyote, and now he, as a human boy, has come to educate you in their ways. He could only have come to you because of what you've done—your killing, your remorse, and your acknowledgment of it that is breaking you open. You are to let him educate you in the ways of his people. You are related."

Then Emma slowly turns to face Anna.

"And you, Anna. Coyote came to you to die."

Anna locks eyes with her. Jesus, who are you? she thinks.

The women look around the circle, then back at Emma. Something has sprung up between them all now, the women, the dead coyote, her killer, the night, Emma's words.

She breaks down now, the woman who killed the coyote in order to protect her sheep. No one touches her or offers comfort, but let her feel what she has done to the coyote and to herself.

Her sobs subside and they know then they are complete. The women stand and gather round the body of the coyote. Lifting her gently, they lower her into the grave. Earlier, Anna lined the hole with boughs of evergreens and now the bowls of corn meal and tobacco are passed hand to hand, each woman sprinkling some into the grave, some with tears, some dry eyed, some mumbling prayers, some singing. And just then, the coyotes over the hill, her pack, begin to howl.

THE NEXT DAY BEGINS clear and bright, but by afternoon clouds gather up and hover low, signaling a snow coming. Anna spends the day stacking wood and making soup she can heat up on the wood stove should she lose power. Adam calls to make sure she's all set, something he does every storm even though she's been widowed for years and is accustomed, if not resigned, to facing all kinds of tempests alone. She tries not to be terse with him, tells him she's fine.

She carries her father and the coyote throughout the day. Their faces superimpose while she chops carrots. Two deaths, two poisons. Two old women—no, she realizes, remembering Emma—three old woman. Two fires. Her handkerchief makes the journey from her pocket to her tears many times. The roots of war run deep, she thinks. Her father was collateral damage in the war against mosquitos and polio, but something else, too, something they both share, these deaths. A battle of control, a war against the wild unknown, a war on coyote hunger. And mosquito hunger. But finally, isn't it a war on the fear of the wild realm of death?

Anna wants redemption for their suffering, and if she understands this, it means that she has to make something beautiful from what she now carries. This irritates her. I don't want any more damn challenges, she thinks, and what fucking good will that beauty do the coyote. It has to be more than beauty. Has to be.

The snow blows and squalls down all evening and all night long. She sleeps a dreamless depth, blank like the snow-covered landscape, and wakes feeling refreshed and grateful for the rest from the wildness of the last few days. The snow covers the humps of boulders in the yard, transforming them into white glittering buffalos. Two shiny black birds ride the humps, flinging snow and looking for seed. Anna smiles at the reliable antics of crows.

She spends the day shoveling snow and sifting thoughts, bit by bit.

She even goes into the woods just at the edge where they buried the coyote and shovels a bit of snow off the grave. Why she does this, for heaven's sake, she doesn't know. "Emma said you came to me to die. What do you want from me? What are you trying to tell me?" The particular silence of deep snow is a hush so complete that Anna's mind quiets and opens.

She returns to the house, grabs her snowshoes, some almonds, and a small thermos of coffee and heads out into the pine forest at the top of the hill where she stands beneath the bowed, snow laden branches of the hemlock, everything settling down in her, dropping to earth. Home.

THAT NIGHT ANNA dreams of
communion wafers round and white and tasteless. She steps up to the altar as she did when a girl. "Body of earthly sorrows," intones the old woman placing the wafer on Anna's tongue, "body of whale . . . body of eagle . . . body of redwood . . . body of . . . body of . . . body of. . ," she murmurs as she moves down a seemingly endless line of people awaiting the wafer of redemption,

reciting a long litany of the lost and disappearing, "body of bison, body of bat, body of coyote . . . ."

The wafer dissolves on her tongue, her own body dissolves then swells into prairie, mountain and forest, desert, swamp and sea, her tissues rip and tear, her bones break, crunching under the terrible pressure of receiving and being so many . . . body of . . . body of . . . body of . . . the soft murmuring litany continues on and on, populating the earth she has become. Fangs spring through her gums, she grows scale, feather, fur, and hide. All around her she hears the rending of human flesh, the shifting swelling earth until, completely dismembered now, in a kind of agony, her heart, the only thing left at the center of her, explodes in a torrent of loss so acute that she is sure she is dying. She floats in her own blood, the life ebbing out of her, and prays for release. For death.

"Oh no!" thunders the old woman. "Redemption is round like the basket, like the urn, like the earth. You've been shown the way. Reenter the hoop, remember the dead."

"We didn't mean it to happen in this way."

"Well, what did you mean?"

"We're afraid."

"And of what are you afraid?"

"Of knowing what and who we've lost and what we've done."

"As well you should be."

She knows then just how terrible is her people's unacknowledged grief.

The old woman leans close, growls low in her ear, "Now the reckoning."

A fierce pounding on the front door wakens her. It's Adam, his voice full of fear and anger. "Anna! goddamn it let me in, Anna!" He stops and she hears his boots crunching through the snow around to the back of the house.

She isn't sure just what world she's in as her body shudders, drenched in sweat, tears running down into an already soaked pillow, her pelvis sore and wrenched. Round, she thinks, hoop, she thinks, redemption is round, the words already fading, grief and reckoning, grief and remembering the dead . . . reckoning.

Adam is back now, renewing his efforts. She lies in the bed, listening to him, his urgency. She has just been spared and he is likely worried that she's dead.

She understands suddenly that the old woman was sitting at the fire on the threshold between the worlds, watching, seeing everything. Everything coming, everything going. A role call of the living, the dead and the dying, holding it all within the circle. Vigil.

Then she understands that Adam has watched her with a similar devotion. She gets up, draws on her robe, and limps down the cold stairs and opens the door. He falls in the door right on all fours while she looks down at him with a kind of amazed curiosity. He knows better than to apologize, which wouldn't wash with the Anna he knows. Instead, he leaps up with a spring that is unnatural and rests his black eyes on her, his gaze nailing her to the floor. "Jesus, you look like hell. I been calling and calling and now I've been banging on this door after taking a look around the property and what's happened here and I got worried about you."

Curious now, she asks, "What do you mean?"

"Well, go put some clothes on and come see for yourself."

Irritated by his concern, but trusting him, she again goes up the stairs to pull on some clothes, realizing her joints ache and her flesh is tender to the touch as she shoves her legs into jeans and boots and a warm pullover. She descends, pulls on a parka and goes out into the woods with Adam.

He leads her to the site of the coyote grave and points. The snow is tamped down into a circle, like a deer bed, at the center of which is the urn, the photo of her father's eyes and, its blood infusing the surrounding snow, the fresh haunch of a goat.

Stunned, Anna contemplates this awful yet deliberate message. Dread rises in her when she hears the receding call of the pack just over the hill. She bolts the path back to the goat barn, sees the tunnel dug underneath, rips open the door casting light on the three mute and terrified goats who stand over the bloody body of the young buck.

In anguish, Anna falls to her knees, wailing.

The goats nervously bend down and sniff her hair as she settles her body on the dead goat's body and cries. Eventually she quiets and listens to herself breathe. Adam stands at the door knowing better than to approach or comfort.

She rocks back and forth, "What have we done, what have we done?"

Now she knows. Coyotes grieve.

She gets up and, like a woman driven, takes the buck's front legs, pulls him out over the snow and into the woods. Adam follows her, but she won't let him help.

"We should bury him."

"No, Adam, they took him. It was an exchange."

"What the hell, Anna?"

"I don't know. I just know they are showing me something, some way to right things."

"Revenge doesn't seem a way to right things to me."

She turns her eyes on him and he shuts up. She bends down and puts her hands on her beloved goat.

"See these puncture wounds on his throat? He was killed quickly with little suffering. You know it wasn't like that for the poisoned coyote. She suffered terribly. It's not revenge, it's something else."

She asks him for some of his tobacco and with shaking hands she sprinkles it on the buck and prays for a good journey, thanking him for his life and love. For several moments, she lays her head against his forehead, then reluctantly rises to leave. She and Adam walk back to the house, turn and sit on the edge of the porch. The goats stand now at the fence, looking to her for reassurance.

She is thick in it now. She doesn't understand but she knows. There is no turning back. "The same thing that killed my father killed the coyote and is killing us. And we're holding the gun. But the death that took this goat, it isn't the same. It's the way of earth. They could have taken his body away, but they didn't. Why? I think it's because I had to make an offering, don't you see? I had to agree to the way of earth. I am the way of earth. We all are. Otherwise the same old war will go on and on. But still, I don't know if I have the courage, I don't think I do."

Spent, she turns to him, "Come in for coffee, Adam," and he does, building the fire while she grinds the beans in her hand crank, grateful for the reprieve from having to explain, from his quick need to get to the bottom of things. Then she buys more time by mixing up a potion of molasses solution for the shaken and skittery goats, puts it in a bucket and brings it out to them, spends a few minutes soothing and sitting and crying while the coffee perks.

She fills the hole back in at the back of the barn, rakes out the bloody hay and replaces it with fresh. She knows it will take time for all of them to adjust, but she also suspects they know more of what has happened here than she does.

"It all started with the ashes, I suppose." She sits stiff and shivering in the rocking chair, clutching the hot coffee mug, talking to him but staring out the window. "My brother was cleaning out the basement and came across the urn with a note for me from my mother."

For Anna when I'm gone.

"I opened the note asking me for forgiveness and leaving me the ashes. I knew it was the past. And so, I thought, fuck it, she burned it and I'll bury it. And fuck forgiveness too. But the ashes wouldn't be buried. I mean, swear to god, Adam, I'd bury the thing, go do some chores and I'd find the urn poking up from the hole. I thought at first that it was the work of some trickster squirrel or some kind of frost heave, so after going through that a couple of times, I got really mad, afraid, too, so I buried it in a rage, determined it would stay buried."

Adam doesn't respond and Anna turns to see him looking at her with a kind of patient worry as if he can't quite square this story with the Anna he knows, that she's lost her good sense or there is something here he's not sure he wants to know.

"Yes, I know," she says. "But I'm telling you that urn did fly through the air, thunked me on the back, landed at my feet, and when I looked down there was a singed photo of my father's eyes staring up at me from the snow. Somebody or something is after me, Adam. I thought it was a demon but I'm beginning to understand it's a goddamned angel."

She sees him smile at the typical pairing of the profane and profound that peppers her speech, and then he takes his soapstone pipe from his jacket pocket, fills it, tamps it, and sucks it into life. The sweet aroma makes her think of her tobacco-growing grandfather and walking barefoot in his plowed fields. Grandpa Joe is in that urn, too, she knows. And Ireland too. She gets up to pour more coffee. Restless, she stands at the window and looks out at the body of her young buck lying in the snow. Her heart is swollen and bruised. She feels suspended as though in a waking dream, yet she's known this feeling before, long ago.

"Since I was a kid, I've wanted redemption. There is something so compelling about the word but I don't know what it means. I've never thought about it in the religious way. It's more like a kind of do-over. There was a feeling always that I needed, or my family needed, to be brought back into life. As though we had somehow landed outside and we couldn't get back in. I didn't know my grandparents, my father's parents were dead when I was born and my mother's parents never spoke about where they came from, their parents, their lives. No stories of what was behind us to carry us forward. You know?" She turns to Adam and then back to the buck.

"Did you know that sin means estrangement from god?"

"You'd think with my name I'd know something about that wouldn't you?" he says. "No, I didn't know that."

"Someone once said that redemption is making something useful or beautiful out of suffering. But how do we make something useful out of the coyote's suffering, or my father's for that matter? Besides, it's too easy. Too easy in some way. And it doesn't heal them or bring them back or change what happened. But if sin is estrangement from what we call god, then redemption is coming home to what we call god. Redemption would be returning to what we're estranged from, right? I mean, I didn't sin against god when I was a kid, whatever kind of god I believed in, I was just a child. But I was outside, we all were. We are all outside something."

She stops to fill the stove. Adam, a man of few words, sits and waits, considers what she is trying to tell him. She goes to the kitchen, pulls open a drawer and rummages around for her old pipe. Finding it, she hands it to Adam to fill. The birch logs flare up and crackle, filling the silence.

"When my father died, we didn't speak of it. We didn't grieve together or tell stories about him. We all went our separate ways. We were outside something. Or maybe the way we didn't grieve means we were already outside, but now we were really far flung, orbiting alone. And I've always had that feeling that something, someone wants back in, needs back in. Without that, I'm lost, and we're lost. That's redemption, I guess. Except the coming back in. There's a price."

She realizes she hasn't told Adam last night's dream, that she's working it out in his presence, and stops herself. Too raw yet to lay before another. So they sit for a bit and then she asks him to leave, that she needs time to—well, she doesn't know really—but time.

She walks him out so she can check on the goats, too, and surprising them both, she thanks him for his devotion to her well-being all these years, for persisting, which embarrasses and pleases him. He instinctively reaches for her and before her fear can restrain her, she lets him. In an inchoate way, she understands that she has to let him, that redemption lies there and if she is meant to live on the periphery, she needn't go without a pack. She sniffs him out—his body is hard with work and he smells of sap and tobacco and fresh air. He smells like trust. They part and look at each other with a kind intensity they both understand.

Anna checks on the goats and returns to the house, pours some fresh coffee, relights her pipe and sits by the hearth, looking out the north window up to the woods where the buck's body lies atop the coyote's grave. She sits for a long time, rocking, thinking, and waiting. She knows it's not over. Exhausted, she falls into a light drowse.

"ANNA."

She senses his presence beside her where Adam sat not so long ago, or is it a lifetime? She wonders fleetingly if she should be frightened, not of him, but of losing herself so completely that she'll go mad. Her body is not hers anymore, it seems, nor her mind. Too permeable, too elastic to hold her shape. Can she endure?

"I know you're having a hell of a time of it aren't you, Anna? It's a bit like dying." The cadence of his voice is slow and gentling. A voice one uses to calm horses. Not the voice she remembers. This is the voice of another time, another place, full of just how it is.

She rests her eyes on him, his presence a quenching rain to the moist yet still parched earth of her heart. Deciding not to question her sanity, she soaks him in, sighing.

"You're here."

"Ay yuh."

"Ay yuh," she repeats softly.

His eyes are dark and tender in a young face. He wears khakis like in the picture, a pack of Chesterfields sticking above his pocket. In her nervousness she wants to crack a joke about that, but holds her tongue.

"Been here all along, Anna. Waiting."

She looks at him, turns to the window and back again, thinking.

"Why now, Daddy? Why all this now, when I'm old?"

"So you could become the woman who believes, Anna, who can carry me. That takes some doing. And I had to become the one worth carrying. That took some doing too."

She gets up from the rocking chair and puts a log into the fire, its pop and sizzle a living song, warming the space around them.

He leans close to the stove, extends his hands for warmth. "I always love to burn the silver birch."

"You mean you loved to."

He laughs. "Well that, too."

Puzzled, she concedes that she, too, loves to burn the birch.

The air shifts, gathering in around them something close yet ineffable, a solemnity almost holy.

"You're the one, Anna," he whispers in answer to her unspoken question. "Look around you. I've been gone from this land of forgetting for a long time. See anyone else trying to remember me?"

She looks at his hands, so like hers, so like her brothers' hands.

"No. Too painful. Agonizing, really."

"Oh, I know, Anna."

"But I couldn't forget, no matter how hard I tried. And I did try."

"That is not entirely of your own doing."

"Yes, I'm beginning to suspect that. An old woman in a dream told me to stop drumming for you. I'm not even sure what drumming for you means. It seemed like a way to remember you. I told her I carry your death in my basket and then she said, 'Everyone here drums for themselves,' and so I stopped. But now," her voice rises with frustration, "*you're* saying I'm to carry you."

He pulls a cigarette from the pack, lights up. Considers. "I know the old woman and we do what she says. But you don't understand. She's stating the problem, is all."

"Which is?"

"That everyone in the realm where you live is drumming for themselves. You're not seeing life properly. You think it's a random thing hurtling toward nothing, full of shards, isolated pieces and then . . . death. End of the road. It's lamentable. And you're all so damn lonely. And afraid. But life is an alive, pulsating thing, Anna, returning to itself again and again, full of mystery.

"I died, yes. The coyote died. Assuming it's the end, you're caught between longing for the past and numbing out your grief. Not just you, you've all forgotten how it is. You're all staggering under the burden of grief that you refuse to know."

"That's what the old woman said."

"But that's not carrying me."

"But I was drumming *for* you."

"Yes, and your remembering is a fragile thread between us. But with all respect, it's a nice idea, but you can't drum for me until you know I'm here. It's an entirely different kettle of fish. You are longing for me, trying to keep me alive. I need you to grieve me, Anna, let me go. So then we can get on with it. *Carry* me. And I will carry you."

She leans back in the chair and gazes out the window. There in the distance her beloved goat lies atop the coyote grave. Near his body sits the urn. The crows perch on the boulder. She gathers in all the dreams, the urn, the old woman's words—life is round, like the basket, like the hoop, like the urn.

"I understand it took some doing."

He smiles. "On both our parts, yes. You know the coyote and me, we died when and how we did because of the thing that is trying to stop the round. So many have been killed in this way. There's all kinds of poison."

She listens, her brow furrowed, resisting the need to fling herself into his arms, afraid somehow she'll fall right through him into air.

"I don't understand," she says. "I see glimmers, but like when I was a kid trying to catch a trout with my bare hands, it flashes in the light, I cup my hands, I have it and then it slips from me and dives and—"

"I know. I know. It's an old way that's hard to redeem in your world. The way to make a kinship with life, not to fight it. But you do remember, Anna, it's in your longing, it dashes by just outside your line of vision. You just have to trust it and follow. The way I trust you."

"You trust me?"

"With my life."

Moved to tears, she looks at him, held by the way he speaks, soft and slow, firm yet warm. Forgiving, a bit like the old woman, and real.

"How can I carry you?"

Her father extends his hand across the space between them. She grabs hold. His hand is callused and hard and warm. "That's right, reach across, Anna. We're right here. We'll carry each other."

In that moment her blood sings an old song, deep in her knowing, and the trout swims willingly into her cupped hands, welcoming her to this feast of the great round, before doubt sends it diving again into the deeps.

"Just tell me, who is we?"

He looks at her with an unvarnished kindness and patience for her long and painful labor.

"Oh, honey, your dead of course."

ANNA ROUSES TO THE GLOWING coals of the diminishing fire, knowing now what she must do.

She puts on her parka and fur hat, warm gloves and boots, lights the kerosene lantern and grabs the shovel from the porch. The gibbous moon hangs full in the east and she stands on the porch making a silent plea for courage. She steps off, shovel over her shoulder while the high held lantern circles her in a soft yellow light, her shadow looming behind her as she walks.

She stops to lean the shovel against the boulder, takes a deep breath and then moves to the coyote's grave where she pauses for a weary, yet taut, moment looking down on the body of her buck. She kneels and lays her hand on the goat's head, a last gesture, before gathering the urn and the photo of her father's eyes. She carries them across the yard where she digs again under the lip of the boulder. She works up a sweat getting below the frost where the earth is dark. Standing for several moments gazing at the photograph, she is hardly able to part with him, struggling to understand something about letting go in order to carry. She opens the lid, puts the photo into the urn and lays it in its final resting place.

She fishes tobacco from her pocket and holds it in the sweaty clench of her hand. Her voice a whisper, "For you, Dad, for you, Ma. For my dear goat and for Coyote, for breaking my heart. For all my dead. I will carry you." She sprinkles the tobacco, leans on the shovel handle, searching for words.

"I know what this asks of me . . . this promise to carry you. I have to come in from the edges. I have to have faith in redemption, in the hoop, like the old woman says. Please help me. I'm afraid. Please help me have the courage to withstand the suffering of remembering."

She pauses. The words do not come easily. She hasn't known how to pray.

"And to speak of what I remember."

Even as she speaks, her fear struggles to overcome her courage, but then she remembers the wracked coyote. Feels the grip of her father's hand in hers and decides. "Fear is poison. Redemption is round. Reenter the hoop. Remember your dead. Fear is poison, redemption is round, reenter the hoop, remember your dead, fear is poison . . . " She covers the urn with black earth.

Taking a deep breath, she turns and walks back to the house, wondering if the urn will stay buried, if she's known the right thing to do. Reaching the porch, she turns and faces the boulder where the urn rests now, undisturbed.

And then they come.

She makes out six of the pack emerging from the shadows into the small clearing, their bodies lowered in a half crouch. They sniff and circle the goat's body, look to where the woman stands then to the goat and back, weighing and deciding. Food or poison?

Anna's heart seizes. She doesn't know if she can bear to witness this rite, the final reckoning the old woman spoke of, a grief, exacting and terrible.

She stands, her hands clenched at her sides, her body shaking as she watches them devour him. She knows it is the way of earth, that he was not hers to give or to withhold, even though it is as though they are eating her own heart.

Finished for now, watching her, the coyotes fling snow over the body and then lie down near the grave, facing her. Something passes between them and she knows that they know the pain she feels because they have felt it too, and that she loves them like they are her own heart.

They rise then to stretch and yawn and open their throats in a yipping chorus, sounding gleefully macabre to Anna's ears. Unrepentant, they laugh, turn, and walk off into the night.

"And now, Anna," says the old woman, "you *must* drum."

The Looking Back Woman
of Scantic Gap

"Memory dies unless it's given a use . . . If one no longer
has land but has the memory of land, then one makes a
map."

Anne Michaels, *Fugitive Pieces*

My name is Sophie Carson and I am a looking back woman. I live at Scantic Gap in the place of the long river, the place where there is a breach of the north-south ledge below the moving water. The place where the water suddenly drops sixty feet, foaming, carrying the force of its descent downstream. It is the place just before change, when the old is done and new is coming. But there is a place there where the water whirls and spirals around, where it rests and considers this change in direction. I like to think it is gathering up memory in that vortex of time, before plunging on.

These are the last words that I leave for you. I leave them because my mother left words for me and I've taken my stick and poked around in those words for nearly thirty years now looking for the bits and pieces of life because I am a scavenger woman, I admit it.

I have spent a lifetime looking down, which is considered the posture of the shamed, the low, which is true I guess in that I learned as a young girl that it is safer to meet earth than to meet eyes. But I would also venture to say that the walk tall, look-straight-ahead posture of many might belie a hatred of dirt. And its secrets.

I am an old woman facing into her death, and I have no living children to leave what truths have come to me. I write them down with the prayer that, lacking an heir to give them to, simply in the writing they find their way into the place where they might be discovered in dream or memory.

Sometimes I lament that we grasp the truth so late and there is no one to tell it to. But if knowledge and memory never die, just

enter the wild circulatory system that is the great round—as my
Grandmother Rayna used to call life, bending down to me, moving
her hands in a pantomime of roundness—well then maybe even a
learning that comes so late and with no one to tell it to is a force
for good, a force for remembering how to be a real human being.

And so, like I said, I took my stick, looking through my
mother's words as if they were bones whose origins hold the
answers to a deep mystery, looking for fragments of field and sky,
a particular earth and people folded into and hidden within the
language of the conqueror, the language I now speak. They say
words came originally from the earth and earth people and that if
we want to dishearten a people into a slow death, first take away
their language. If I sift through her words will I find my people's
bones, the bones that are mine to honor and bury and to build
upon? Will I find memory bones? I do not know, but I believe so.

My way-back people arrived on ships that sailed from their
motherland Scotland, but they were Ulster Scots, which means they
had emigrated to Northern Ireland from Scotland many
generations before sailing to North America. They had been forced
to Ireland by the pressures of poverty and hunger set in motion by
their enemy the English and to North America for the same
reason. They'd been defending their Scotland and their living from
the English for hundreds of years until they had become keen-
bladed weapons used by the English to steal Ireland from the
Catholics. Another hundred years of battle. Again starved out by
the English, they set sail for North America. As a child I never
knew any of this but it was there in my mother's words every Saint
Patrick's day, "You're Orange Irish, never, ever wear green on
Saint Patrick's day, not orange either." She didn't find it necessary
to explain, nor did I ask, being an apprentice to their art of
forgetting.

I am descended from a hard working, hard drinking people.
And hard hearted too, suspicious and battle weary. But if we go
back far enough, my own from across the waters were a long time

ago indigenous peoples who wore skins and lived off the land and the animals. For whom the land and the red deer were sacred. The blights of the potato and the suffocation of their trade in flax that finally brought them here to this country were evils made tangible, growing out of the soil of greed, oppression, and warfare.

You have heard of the potato famine I'm sure. I am here because of a fungus that moved underground killing at the roots a singular crop that was planted only because it was deemed uncivilized to move from place to place, following the sun and the seasons and the game, and besides how could it be good to use only what was killed, or woven, or gathered when some could have more than necessary, and storehouses full of the labor of rough hands not their own, whose fruits were sold so that one's people, god Bless us All, could have more than was needed. I'm here because of a blight of greed that stoked the fire burning nearly everything between first breath and extinction. Some perished, some became the living dead.

And so they came. I am their blood.

I come from people who fled land and kin and dream and root to swell and rock over those vast and mysterious deeps between despair and hope where a future might be born. I lost many, not so much to the rough seas as to that hope. I can see them now, in a desperate effort not to sink, flinging baggage and memory and heartbreak into the deeps, a burial at sea, the people full of fervent faith in resurrection. I see them now—the memories, the ways, the griefs, the stories at the moment when the last of them submerges, the water closing over the surface like scar tissue, I see them floating down to the bottom of the sea. Oh, the sea has known more sorrow that a being should have to hold.

And my people did, oh yes, go on. A kind of resurrection, but it seems to me they rose up as hungry ghosts. If you can't remember where you came from, how do you know who you are? And if you don't know who you are, how do you know how to live? And it seemed they had transformed into what their enemies had made them, killing the people of this land with the relish of a misplaced revenge. And the blood of those people too runs through me. This is life's great irony. Two warring bloods living side by side keeping this life running now for some eighty years. I lost many, not so much to history as to hope. The kind of hope that carries us across seas over borders, that issues from a hunger so desperate it drives murder. Of a people, of a land. Hope can be terminal. It blinds grief, the portal to the soul of a person.

I don't mean to be morbid, and actually I am not. But I am deranged and so aren't you. Like the bear who lives in my memory, I pace in the cages of history's making.

If trying to remember what you've lost is too much for your tender soul, yet remembering is the only way back to being a human being, well then, what hope for life is there except to tie yourself to the mast and endure a sadness beyond enduring? To perhaps die in the effort or chance to resurface with your dear ones—your people, your red deer, your stories, the smell of your land–held close. I have tied myself to the mast as best I can in my long life and I've resurfaced a few times, yes.

These are my relations who I knew and who I carry. My now dead. I am the only daughter of Fiona and Angus, maternal Granddaughter of Rayna and Joe, great Granddaughter of Marie and Brian. I never knew or heard stories of my father's parents, only that they died on the coffin ships coming from Scotland, leaving their sixteen year old son Angus, named for his father's great uncle on the Ulster side, to make his way in this new world. He could be a hard man but I feel a tenderness for his young self. He was taken in and raised by a childless couple, master weavers who taught him. In that, he was lucky.

I am eighty years old this spring. Eighty. I live in the house my father and mother built when I was five years of age. It is a small and pleasing one with windows overlooking the land in all directions, which wasn't at all practical at the time, but my mother couldn't be boxed in. She insisted on light and Angus did as she asked. There are two windows in each wall, looking east, south, north, and west. The first floor is one large square room and a sleeping loft occupies the second floor with small windows at the gable ends and along the upper side walls to let in the light. Many years ago now we put in gas lighting. A small woodstove sits in the northwest corner and a cooking stove on the south wall which I also run with gas. The man comes to replace my tanks on a regular basis and is always trying to talk me into bettering my conditions, which to me are quite fine. I'm warm, I'm fed, and I'm held by the dead of the very same trees standing all around the house. We are both old now, that wood and me, burnished and creaking.

There is a two-hearthed fireplace in the center, facing south and north where my mother once cooked our meals in the large black kettle that still hangs there from a swinging hook. I look out on slender white birches and the garden where, when a younger woman, I planted corn every year, just enough for me to put up for the winter and for anyone else who foraged through. We seemed to work it out, my friends and I, but now things being so much more crowded people have to use electric fences and other torturous methods to feed only themselves. I still put in a few ears for old time's sake. I would miss the beloved corn too badly if I didn't.

I write this sitting at my mother's writing desk, snug up to the windows that overlook the Gap. While I can't see the water, it being too far down and the drop-off a distance of some thirty yards, its voice is as inseparable from me as my own thoughts. The moving water a thrum underlying all my days here.

A hundred years before I was born, a dam was built to harness all that frothing power for industry. Good luck, I say.

I've always felt it right that I live here in the Gap, the space where time moves and stands still perpetually. They say Scantic is an Indian word for fork. So I live at the gap in a river that demands a decision, a kind of crossroads. But I have resisted this, staying put, some would say eddying around in circles, living in the whirlpool of memory. But I would say, I am living in the whirlpool of remembering, unwilling to move on until I remember enough to know where I'm going.

When I was a girl I took it as my job to keep the sludge and backup cleared at the dam where I live. Every day, with a stick taller than me, I'd move it along, so that the water could go home, carrying its stories downstream, messages smuggled through the forces that would keep it back.

If I thought that my death was the end of life, I wouldn't bother. But I know it isn't so, that all my seeming to go round in circles is making a way and will continue to make a way is my conviction. I am, by my reckoning, neither insane or demented. You may decide differently. But this is what I know.

Forgetting is the madness. I have looked my whole life for what carries the remembering and I know that memory is like the trout that abides in cold slumber during the winters of our forgetting. Fish can wait, have that way of submerging when the cold heart sweeps over the water, have that way of waiting for the one, as fish kind have done in the far away past, the one to whom it will offer itself, the one who will read it all in the pink interior of gill, the soft bone hieroglyphs articulating the story of time and water, moon and tree and bear and the dead at the bottom of the sea—the one who will eat and remember the return and all that it asks. Memory can wait a long time—it is faithful like that. Like our death. Like the fish, like the bones.

Memories don't present themselves sharp and clear, but arise in shadow and light-filled water, emerging and disappearing in the flickering thrown by the dance between sun and swaying trees. This is why you must always keep good vision out of the corner of your eyes. You won't find everything you need to know in straight ahead history books, unless you know to read between the lines where another kind of truth is secreted. History is facts, remembering is a place, a story, a portal.

WHEN THE DUCKS CAME, the day opened out before me new and spring green after a long snow-heavy winter. The smell of birth was in the air—the scent of water released from its long sleep, free to wander, to travel carried by clouds, free to pour down its winter dreams onto a new land, taken in by the warming trees anxious for news from elsewhere. Spring, it said, spring, and the sap ran. Never curse the rain.

Young ferns spiraled tight and hairy out of breaking ground, driven by some secret inner timing in relation to earth and sun and water and dark they will unfurl, generous and new, open hearted and unashamed in their beauty like small children who remember where they come from.

In the north end of the clearing, I'd put out my mice-tested supply of corn from last year's harvest for the deer after such a long cold. Some I plant, some I share. When they flew in, oh, not the deer, the mallards—imagine flying deer, I'd love to see that, or would I? Just as unnatural as so much that is spawning now. This reminds me of my Grandfather Joe, "The devil spawn," he used to say, declaring something or someone as unholy. I don't believe in the devil, and spawn is a perfectly good word, but the phrase can still run cold all over me.

I have lived here almost my whole life and I've never seen ducks on this land. I live far above the river's turbulent gap and there is no water here where my house is set. Seeing them doesn't seem natural to me, yet I am glad all the same to be witness to the emerald plumage of the male as he faithfully bobs, waddles, and gabs alongside his more sedate and muted mate. In my mind, I flew up and imagined the bright yellow pool from the sky against the drabness of an early cold spring drawing them down to investigate.

But this is what I really want you to know—when the ducks came, I thought to myself, this is the year I will die. And then, they're deranged. The thoughts flew in as suddenly as the ducks, taking my breath, then my attention, my curiosity. Then I remembered—there it was, whole, in every sense. I felt my hand clasped in my mother's, the relaxed weight of my small arm pulled up by her greater height. The hot sun on my body, standing, the two of us, united, staring between the bars. Were we inside looking out, or outside looking in? I would not have known to ask it then, but now I know the answer. Both. If I close my eyes and get very still I can smell the hot sun on pavement baking spilled popcorn, mingled with the acrid tinge of cooked piss and musky fear, the light gleaming on the moving white and yellow fur. People parading past behind us, women pushing strollers, kids carrying balloons. Her snout bleeding, weeping always, she paced from side to side, running her nose along the bars, back and forth, her head always facing those who watched, those of us who gawked with pity and curiosity. How did we stand her apparent agony? We did. We returned again and again as persistent as her pacing. My hand in mother's hand, me asking, "What's wrong with that bear?" and after a considered pause, her answering, "She's deranged."

That was some seventy years ago and yet it has stuck in me, waiting and devoted turning up at just this moment. Deranged. Today I weep for that bear, when back then it seemed she solicited only my curiosity. But I am an old woman now and I understand that I have been pacing with that homeless bear for most of my life. Companions in our derangement.

Like the bear, I am trying to walk home and it is hopeless. I do not recommend it, but I do encourage it. I wake everyday in homesickness and while I don't remember the way, I keep the homesickness alive because it is the only entry I have that might lead me into the way it should be. I may not get there, but I keep it open for you, or for someone who comes behind you.

I feel that persistent searching in my own self, the looking for a thing remembered but not storied. A mourning with no name, a searching in the darkness of forgetting. The bear remembered with her body, though. She wanted to go home and she was going to walk there, and in the walking maybe forgetting the way and thus the pain, which is just as well because she couldn't go home. There was no return.

No return. Is this hell, then, a deep remembering with no way to return? But then it came to me that perhaps the ducks have returned, perhaps a long time ago there was water here on this land and at this particular moment in their particular flight they were drawn down by ancient memory still alive, dormant until all the various and mysterious conditions of its awakening wove the pattern of return, of remembering.

Consider this. I take this as more confirmation of what I know about remembering. If they can remember, then so we can, too, and maybe in that there is some way, some ancient track laid down in the same place that you found this testament that I've left. Perhaps everything is there if we make ourselves open. Perhaps in all derangement there is a clue, a hidden door. When my mother said that to me many years ago, it was a teaching so hidden and so obvious that it took me a long time to find it. And is my looking back a door, neither nostalgia nor sentimentality but . . . well, a turkey hen I knew once comes to mind. Many years ago I watched her walking through the clearing and up into the woods with her brood. At the edge she stopped and stood, looking back, waiting on a slow adventurous poult lollygagging behind. Perhaps I am the hen looking back, tending the new life, or maybe I am the poult, saying, where *are* you, to those gone.

Some are driven insane by the attempt to forget, and some seem insane trying to remember. I suspect this is what the thing they call dementia is about. There seems to be an epidemic of only being able to remember the past. Is this life's way of turning our faces towards that which has been buried inside of us? Perhaps the insane and the demented are truly our doorways to a kind of salvage.

I know this, too, that the ones on top will try to convince us that we began in primitive conditions, that our hearts were brutal and that now we're civilized. The more civilized we've become, I see this in my short life, the more brutal. Zoos are civilized. I know that if we go deep enough and far enough back we will find the human beings we were. Can we bear it, is the question.

THIS MORNING I GOT UP, made myself a strong coffee, and watched the dark pull back, revealing a woods suspended in fog. A Scotch mist. That's what they called it, my folks. Sometime ago I read a line in a poem—*a drizzle as fine as fish bones*—and I thought of my dead father then and his trout fishing in a rain as fine as needles, stinging and enlivening on the skin. A waking up rain.

The sun rose and burned through the fog, everything shone with brilliant clarity. Drops of water containing the whole world hung from blades of grass and I felt washed clean. I was born in spring, on just such a day, and have always thought it a good season to migrate down my mother's muscular canal into the capable hands of my Grandmother Rayna.

My mother suffered the birth. It tore her apart and maybe that's why I was the first and the last born.

And so I was handed to Rayna from the beginning. My first memories are of her dirt-encrusted leathery heels, alternately landing and disappearing into her long skirts as I anxiously crawled along behind, relieved each time her foot descended, only to be quickly dismayed as the other lifted and disappeared. In time, I came to trust this here-now-gone rhythm that guided my days, extending that understanding to life's events and various migrations. One could even go so far as to say that Rayna's large flat feet shaped an understanding that has guided me my whole life. Yes, one could go that far. I remember I would sometimes sit at her feet, my back firmly against whatever stoop or chair she perched upon, shelling peas or smoking her pipe. I can still see my little brown hands hanging onto her big toe or laying calmly on her big brown foot while she sang me church hymns.

Rayna was the daughter of Marie, an Abenaki woman, and Brian, a Highland Scot come to Canada for the fur trade with the

Northwest Co. He'd been wandering and trapping when he met Marie, the daughter of traders in what is now far eastern Maine up near what became the Canadian border. When the fur trade 'declined'—meaning when the animals had all been killed by greed like they tried to do to the Indians and nearly did—Marie and Brian moved south to New Hampshire to work in the mills. Rayna was born there, one of ten children, five of whom lived to adulthood. Her husband Joe, an Ulster Scot who had emigrated to the states to work as a weaver, met Rayna at a church function and fell in love with her handwoven baskets, is what he always said. A skill she learned from her mother. They were beautiful and useful baskets, woven with prayers in a language I never learned. He told me many times that his proposal to Rayna was, "I'll cut down ash trees for the rest of my life for you." It was then understood that the weaver and the basketmaker would wed.

And so my mother Fiona was born there in New Hampshire, one of five children. Between disease and calamity she was the only one to survive to adulthood. She lost her brother Fergus to the soft ice when he was fifteen. The others were infant deaths from diphtheria. I remember going to the cemetery with my Grandmother to visit the tiny white gravestones, lined up like sweet baby's teeth, where we would leave ears of corn and flowers from her garden. Rayna carried her grief so quietly that when I asked her one day was she sad about her babies, she told me that yes she was sad but that she had a secret to tell me—"Everything is round, Sophie, and nothing dies and their spirits have to be fed." And so I asked her was she feeding her babies corn and flowers then? She just nodded.

I only know Rayna was a mixed blood Abenaki-Scot woman because my father disliked her so much he couldn't keep quiet about her ways. Rayna being my mother's mother, Fiona of course carried Abenaki blood. But my father adored my mother and so he ignored that fact of her origins.

71

Rayna was a Christian woman, educated through high school and a lover of books. But refusing to forget who she carried in her blood, she resisted my father's efforts to erase her. And because Fiona was her only living child, I suspect that she tried to instill in Fiona what she could of her people's ways, the ones that hadn't been purged from her. Rayna caught fish with her bare hands and didn't wear shoes unless it was too cold, and even then she wore soft-soled leather boots, though my mother pleaded otherwise. And she rose every morning before dawn to greet the sun. My mother had long since given up such magic for the love of my father. And I suspect removing her from Rayna was one of Angus's aims in migrating down to Scantic Gap when I was five. But you see, again, this left me without a useable past. Until I pieced it together as a young woman, I knew nothing of our Ulster history, believing that we had all sprouted from this land right here, even though, in my eyes, Rayna seemed the only one who knew how it is supposed to be. Even my Grandpa Joe believed in her wholly and they were the only ones I could tie myself to. My small self trusted them completely. My Scots-Irish father had long ago fallen victim to the great forgetting and took my mother with him. What kind of love is that, when turning against your deepest self and all your dead is a love offering?

Angus worked in the weaving mills for several years—oh, the Scots were good weavers, legendary. But after a while, trying to escape a life of lung disease and deadening work and having pinched enough money together, my parents bought three acres of land where my father commenced tobacco farming. And where I tried to forget my Grandparents and all we'd left behind and to get along. And so for a while I, too, became a hungry ghost, driven by my own emptiness, haunting the hollows of Scantic Gap looking for I knew not what. This, I believe, is what threw me into the arms of Samuel—that and a certain curve to his hip, but that's for later.

I WOKE TODAY to the memory of the ducks visit yesterday and the pacing bear. Is this the year I will die? Well, if so, no time to waste then. I got up, dressed and made coffee as the dark pulled back revealing another foggy morning. I remembered my father then getting up early to fish and returning in the late afternoon. He'd sit on the back porch stoop, a shimmering trout laid out neatly on the newspaper he put down to hold the guts, the neat slit up the middle, the quivering silky pink interior as he fileted and lifted out the fine bones, some of which escaped detection making the meal a rather dire feast of warnings, don't choke on the bones! which always conjured the death scene of a small child—me!—clutching her throat, dying over a plate painted by some Dutch realist, the bones and flesh of the fish laid across a delft blue platter.

My father must be around me these days, as I keep remembering him. Maybe he's come to get me?

I carry my coffee down to the bench on cliff's edge to watch the water plunge over the gap down below, thinking of Rayna and how she would catch fish by crouching low in the shallows, whispering in a voice quiet and reassuring, waiting.

Maybe I didn't remember her voice all those years I was away from her because Rayna didn't say much, or ever talk too loud, a complaint often voiced by my father, Angus. Not understanding the sudden uprooting, I longed for her, searching for her everywhere until I came to understand that for me her voice and face had dissolved into everything peaceful and calm and direct—in the sough of the pines, in all that is quiet yet speaks powerfully with a round assurance of what is underneath the masks and disguises of a people gone mad with forgetting. My people. Maddened with forgetting.

My father's distaste for Rayna, and my mother's masked shame, spoke to their own lineage—having had to turn away from everything that held them. They learned to stand in "I am not that" rather than in the more deeply rooted, "This is who I am and these are my people." Knowing who you are by declaring what you're not, how crazy is that? It leads to all kinds of suffering. It seemed Grandma Rayna would always be a stranger to my father. He had to keep her that way so he had a place to stand. Pretty shaky ground, don't you think? But one couldn't speak of it, none of it.

I learned to watch then, to attend to what was not said, and found it a reliable way to remember and to know. So, you see, remembering isn't always in the facts. It's in the bones. It's in the instincts and the old stories if you're diligent enough to unearth them. Sometimes it's in the particular strangeness that is you. I've come to trust that the peculiarities that I carry are given to me by my dead. But you have to stay in practice, you know. You have to become a good tracker, to ferret out and remember the stories told to you and the stories of your own life.

That's why I share these things with you, because I don't know what might emerge from them years from now, what remembering might be birthed in you by the stories you will carry from me and your own life, like the ducks returning. At the very least, you might consider the necessity of developing the way of noticing, remembering so that it is at the ready when the time comes, because it will come.

I FINISHED MY COFFEE and just when I'd gathered myself up to begin preparations for fishing, in swooped the mallard pair! All wing and conversation, landing not ten feet from me, then waddling off to the corn. "What're you doing here?" I asked them. They gave me the eye like I was the one trespassing, decided I was okay, and turned back to their business.

First I fed the goats, Farley and Kate, my two dear companions, who are quite taken with the ducks. They being too old for breeding, and my hands too arthritic for milking, Farley and Kate are retired now. Kicked back and enjoying the goings on at the Gap, never bored. I've always loved goats, since I was a kid. Back then, during harvest, Angus and Fiona brought me over to the Dixon's farm for watching while they worked the fields. Roxie and Carrie, an older childless couple, loved me and I loved being there. "Well Sophie," Carrie would say, bending down to be eye to eye "what're we gonna do today on the farm?" Then we'd make the rounds collecting eggs from broody hens, picking blueberries before the birds got them. But the goats, saved to last, were my favorite. There was a mysterious affinity between us—even the most ornery goat loved me. That's one of those peculiarities one should notice. I smelt so bad of buck that when my parents came to pick me up they rolled their eyes and pinched their noses. It was a ritual scolding about those dirty animals.

Oh well, you can't fight fate, nor should you knuckle under to it. Fate demands a good wrestling.

I take my tackle basket, woven by Rayna for my father. I always wondered about that. Why did she weave a fishing basket for someone who clearly didn't like her, and ridiculed her ways? Some would say it's the Indian way. The old stories abound up there about how the Indians greeted the white people with a unfathomable generosity. Which both made them curious to the whites but also contemptible to people who had fought for every scrap they had for hundreds of years.

I've come to understand that weaving the basket was Rayna's way of being generous, a gift above suspicion, while at the same time bushwhacking my father with surprise—being a fisher of unparalleled pride and skill he couldn't refuse what he knew to be not just a tackle basket, but an auspicious and powerful magic communicating with the canny trout. When he carried that basket, he'd come home with enough fish to dry and salt in good supply. And I suspect he understood that it wasn't just his skill, although you'd never catch him owning up to that.

Leaving my shoes on the shore, I wade into the water using the small slippery stones as steps and make my way to the large grey boulder I've fished from since I was a small girl. This river, who carries the memory of ice and snow from the cold lands up north on its journey south to the gulf sea, has rocked me nearly my whole life. She knows me by now, and the fish probably do, too. I believe the river and I are friends, and I trust it completely. I'm not so sure about the fish, although I am a good fisher, too, and try not to inflict any more suffering than I need to in order to catch my dinner. I bait the hook with bacon, throw my line, giving it enough slack for it to carry down river.

This is how I do it. I first slow my breath, then softening my gaze I enter the cold, golden water with my mind, until the river not so much forgets I'm here, as embraces me the way an old being might embrace a young one.

It is lovely. The rain has long stopped, the fog lifted. The sky is still overcast blue metal, the new green brilliant against it. False hellebore grows along the banks. I always loved their pleated leaves, like fancy dresses.

I lean back against the boulder, waiting, thinking about Rayna and Angus. And Samuel.

I've lived here on this river since we migrated from up north, and lived in Angus's and Fiona's house nearly all my life with a ten year foray into marriage and motherhood that undid me but might have also been the making of me.

Samuel was a worker on Angus's farm, fresh off the boat from County Armagh, assured a job by Angus before he set foot on ship. He was twenty years old when I first laid eyes on him, but to be honest it was his hips I noticed first. The tilt and swivel of them as he bent to fork the hay, gracefully turning to toss it into the wagon, his damp shirt clinging to the winding path of sweat along his backbone before disappearing into the pants that hung on those hips. I had a wild and sudden thirst for him then and I stood watching until he jumped up into the seat, clucked the horses into action and gave me a cockeyed and knowing grin as he tilted his hat to me on the way to the fields. It was then I noticed he was handsome, too. I was young, just 18, and from that moment my mind and heart determined him to be my magnetic north.

We loved to dance the old dances, reels and jigs and square dancing in the red barn down the way from Scantic Gap. The barn had been raised in the fifty years before I was born and was at one time both church and community hall. And sometimes in the winter it was the cold house, the place where we put our dead when the ground couldn't be melted for burying. Fashioned from hundred-year-old pines, painted in the blood and milk red of the day, the barn surely remembered itself as a living being. When the dancing stopped and the midnight hour was upon us, we could hear the wood groan and creak in the wind, and I swear once I heard the cows calling in the vaulted space above us.

Our favorite caller was Odiah Pease. Carried away by the mother tongue, he called half the time in Gaelic, a language we did not know but responded to nonetheless. Between twirling and stomping and sweating, we ate bannock and drank fermented cider. We courted.

To me, Samuel wasn't only hips and charm. I was sure he carried a poet's heart and my longing for it to be so almost made it true. He grew himself into the image I shined on him, and not knowing what it was that actually possessed him so, he could not resist stepping into the glamor. And I loved him. I loved the smell of him and his hands on my body and the lopsided grin and the sheer possibility of him, still a young man in his blooming. I wanted that bloom right inside of me. I wanted that bloom to plant itself so deep in me that in the planting we would become a wild thing snuffling in the woods, delirious with smells and hot on the trail of the prey that would fulfill all our longing. Well, you can imagine, first we consummated the marriage, then we formalized it. Surely my Presbyterian ancestors turned in their graves. But now I think it made the *really* old ones of all my bloods happy.

Samuel and I got along well as long as things went along well. Mother and father deeded us a small piece of land down the river and up the hill a bit from their house and we built a small house and a little goat barn for my goaties, and we kept a pig and chickens, of course. Samuel was a good-hearted man with a sunny disposition, but not much for storms. Half way into our marriage, the poet I had imagined was wrecked on the shoals of irretrievable loss.

I see as I write this that the crows are gathering in the trees around me, witnesses to sorrow or gleeful omens of death I do not know, but I love them all the same. They endure with good humor, it seems to me. Which I have tried to do. Not cheerfulness, but an unqualified openness to what is and what will come.

We were married for ten years, he working hard at the farming with Angus and I at the home farm. There I carried two children, a boy and a girl. I lost them both in the sixth month. Stillborn. But I claim it as a motherhood all the same, the carrying, the anticipation and the birthing. I held those two dead babies in my hands, Theodore and Anna, and being the looking back woman, I hold them still. They are still mine and I remember them. Like Rayna, I feed them corn and flowers. They are buried right here next to Angus and Fiona and Rayna. Yes, Rayna, but I'll get to that.

FOUR FISH AGREED to come home with me today, nearly leaping into my basket. I brought two down the road to Carl and Rowena and the kids and they welcomed the addition to their meal. They gave me some good lovely potatoes to go with my supper. Carl is a good man. I've known him since he was a baby, his people being originally from Tyrone County as were mine. He and his wife Rowena have four children, ages ten to twenty, the oldest married and carrying her first. Rowena comes to visit often and we sit and speak about life. She weaves the most beautiful blankets from her own wool, sunsets being her speciality. One could do worse than to be born or die under one of Rowena's blankets.

My mouth watered as I made my way home just thinking about those fish. As soon as I got in I loaded up the cooking stove and then cleaned the fish as my father taught me to. I fried them up with the potatoes. They were delicious, the taste of clean river water still in them, and the potato skins tasted of the good earth mixed with salt and butter.

I ate and remembered how when I was a young girl living here on the river, a great hurricane ripped through, washing away the steep banks of the road that ran alongside a small parish church that served as the one room schoolhouse where I went to school. I remember the roar of the wind from down in our potato cellar where we waited out the storm, the smell of the damp earth and roots, the jars of canned goods, the rich, dense colors of plums and tomatoes—purple and red jewels radiating in the light of the lamps. And the quiet after the wind moved on and the rain slowed to a drizzle. We waited still, dreading to see the damage to crop and orchard. When we finally opened the door into the house, sunlight flooded in through the western windows, the last sunlight of the day, that particular golden color of ripe pears, suffusing everything with a burnished and mysterious character, an inner beauty rarely glimpsed in the noon light. But true, I hoped at least, true. I wanted that kind of beauty in myself, in us. I counted on it. I still do.

For days after that storm we cleaned up the land, pruning trees and re-staking what was possible. Canning what was salvageable. Not satisfied with scavenging what lay on the earth, I was always a digger, too, and I couldn't resist wandering off to sift through that dirt newly opened to the elements of sun and wind and my eyes. I can see that girl now, squatting down and digging with her hands, wondering what on earth she was looking for. Now I know to ask, what was looking for me?

There, at the church, I found my first sizable bone. I held it in my young hand with the greed of possession and discovery but when I took it to my mother, she looked at the bone, at me, back to the bone, a flicker of fear crossing her face. I think now I understand she was deciding whether to ignore the incident or not, whether to treat that bone with caution and respect or to dismiss her fear as superstition. Decided, she told me to take it right back where I found it.

I didn't. I kept that bone and when Rayna came to me after my babies died and saw it there on the hearth, she looked at me with pity and I decided she thought their deaths were something to do with the bone, with the theft of it. I felt badly about that but I never asked her. I didn't want to know.

But I had to have that bone. It was proof somehow. Now, whenever I look at it, I think of my long lost dead at the bottom of the sea or deep in the earth and all their dreams and my babies are there too, slipped right through my fingers, or taken. I've considered that my old ones, my grandmothers, had come to claim those babies, taking them into the deeps. The deaths of my babies spoke to me, making clear the claim on the living by the dead. Since then, every day I feed my dead. A prayer, a greeting, food set upon the boulders.

You might think these thoughts are the product of a deranged mind, thus dismissible. Samuel did. But before you dismiss them, too, understand that no one knows better than the deranged mind what it means to lose the very ground we call home. The kind of home that is laid down inside the cells, that makes them sing with knowing the songs and ways of thousands of years. And that only comes from knowing the earth under your feet. It's not just about having an address. If indeed you can resist the seductions of modern life long enough to listen.

When I found that bone, a fragile understanding broke ground in me, that here is solid proof of memory, that the earth remembers us. That the earth remembers everything. I held in my hand the weight and beauty of a life that came before me. When I found that bone it planted in my young mind the seed of time, and that, perhaps, all time comingles and is perhaps knowable. When I found that bone I began to find myself, you see. Do you? I located myself in timelessness.

And when I defied my mother and kept that bone, it was a way to try to keep myself. I know now that if we cannot find ourselves within the thread of time, we are dangerous people who believe our acts are of no consequence. We are the fruition of no one's dream and we do not carry the dream of the future.

Years later, I learned that in all probability that bone was from the burial of a Scantic Indian, distant relations of mine, and I understood the hurricane was memory's breath that day, exposing the bones of a people long buried in the banks of the river that fed and carried them in life and in death.

I take comfort in knowing that the earth I walked to school held the dreaming and story of those who lived here before me. Will it some day hold mine? And does the earth my across-the-seas people left behind hold their memory still, and will it call to me? Is it? I believe so. I am counting on it.

That land had not been lived on since the Indians camped, fished, loved and birthed there. And then, some two hundred years later the storm roared through. And eventually bulldozers, too. And then two men in the 40's, amateur archeologists, also found some bones along that same riverbank.

But of course they got curiouser and curiouser and they dug into those graves, finding fire pits, bone hooks and pot pieces—it was an old fishing village. Well, the men unearthed the bones, disturbed their dreaming, collected them and put them in glass cases, objects of curiosity, relics of a thought-to-be-gone people.

Glass cages. Maybe those men wanted proof, too, and all the people who paraded by those bones, maybe that was their memory trying to surface, the earth trying to pull them back into itself and break the spell of forgetting. But those bones haven't been fed for all these years, and they are hungry.

This is what I believe—those bones have been dreaming for a long time now, from inside their glass prisons they have been dreaming back the voices of the land, the waters, the winds, the disappeared. Seeding the dreams of those who are gutted of memory.

Those old ones are whistling up the winds, speaking to us through the language of a wild imbalance. The nightmares are riding the pain of exile and all that's come of it. I am sure of it. Will we listen? Will we take the medicine? Does anyone know the language?

I PLANTED THE CORN today, the seeds saved out from last year. First I haul a few wheelbarrows of goat compost from the pile and mix it into the soil. I make a hole with my planting stick and then I get down on my knees, hands full of seeds, and move along the row, whispering encouragement. Takes me longer every year, but it's good thinking time.

I birthed Theodore in the winter, and the ground, as frozen as my heart, would not receive him, and so we wrapped him in blankets and canvas and put him in a tiny coffin Samuel built from yellow pine. Samuel worked poetry on that box, carved stalks of wheat into the cover, their heads heavy with seed. We laid him in the goat barn loft. The barn was our cold house that winter and I took comfort in that Theodore would be companioned by the goat's soft bleats and gentle snuffling as they pulled hay from the bin. I would not bring him to the cold house near the church because I didn't want to be that far away from him. Samuel protested, but I won that battle. Men like Samuel are undone by what they can't control and he could not manage my sorrow or the fierce way I stood my ground in it. I have always wanted my dead nearby. Why would we want them anywhere else? It's never made any sense to me.

Samuel thought I was crazed with grief and we quarreled about it. When I look back on it, I was wild with fight, I was taken over with a certainty that wasn't mine. I staked my claim over my boy's tiny and perfect body, over my dear Theodore. I was a woman hewing to an old way that I did not know. I was infiltrated by my risen up dead. From the depths of memory, they seized me like it was their last chance. And, call me crazy, but I suspect it was. There were legions behind me and Samuel felt it. We were going to claim our dead if it was the last thing we did.

I took the shotgun and laid it on the little casket and hauled it on the cart to the goat barn where I waited for the battle. And this, too, I remembered in my bones, this waiting for battle. But it was over. Samuel came to me the next morning, the first rays of sunlight glinting in his worried straw hair, looking for all the world like a small boy himself. And he sat down then and laid his head on my leaking breasts and we wept. The goats gathered around, and, still wailing, we hoisted the coffin up into the loft to await the ground.

We weathered that death. We spoke of Theodore often, what he might have looked like if he had lived. We noted his activity about the place, overturning rocks, picking flowers from the garden. He was real to us. But then the next early winter, I birthed Anna and she, too, was born dead. This time I knew well before the birthing. This time I carried the dead inside me knowingly and it changed me forever. Or maybe it revealed me to myself, and to my people.

There was no argument between Samuel and me this time, no need. Folks thought we had bonded in a kind of mutual madness. They could understand our deviant actions the first time as an insanity brought on by grief, but it was considered civilized by then that the dead are removed from the living and are no longer our business. They are god's business. But I insist that my dead are my business. Still births. I've often thought about that word, still . . . silent, unmoving, but also on-going, still here, they were stillborn and they are still here. Like all our dead.

It was a long hard winter that year and I nearly lost my mind with grief. Worried, and over the objections of my father, Fiona sent for her mother. Rayna came in the spring—the way being clear for her to travel and the ground receptive to the shovel. I hadn't seen her in many years. She was an old woman by then but I could see she was still strong. I loved her so.

Her skin was the softest buttery deer skin and her hair so shockingly white I couldn't take my eyes off it when we first greeted each other. She shyly told me that her mother never had a grey hair on her head. But her father's mother, well . . . running her fingers through her radiant mane, she grinned at the irony of it. "Blood will out, Sophie, never forget that. My skin is my mother's people and my hair speaks of my father's." It seemed to me that Rayna had found her way to come to peace with the two warring peoples inside her. Maybe that's the way love works, as her parents did love one another, her father refusing to leave her mother when trapping was no longer possible, when the fur bearers had been hunted out and nearly decimated, and many trappers hied to home.

After we buried Anna in her tiny box, next to Theodore's grave, Rayna brewed me some dried mugwort tea she had harvested and we sat on the front porch, bundled in blankets against the cold winds of grief because I couldn't bear to be shut up in the house. That afternoon we rocked for hours, the rhythm of the creaking chairs a comfort. Even my cold, numbing body was a comfort to me, imagining the cold underground houses of Anna and Theodore. But my breath betrayed me. Hot and moist and visible, it belied an inner pulsing aliveness. I hated it then, as I watched it issue into the air, perhaps dropping down into the river, carried to some other place. Rayna saw the hatred of my own living breath and it was then she told me.

"You were born in the early morning, Sophie. After a long and hard fought night. Joe and your father sat outside the door praying to their gods while I attended your mother and you, praying to mine. Spring was coming, the new time, and I wondered who you were who fought so hard to live and at the same time fought to return to where you had come from. What would it be, I asked? Then the mallards flew over calling to god the way they do and after that you decided. I could hardly see you for all the blood pouring from my child and I thought for sure that one of you would be dead. But no." She paused then and we rocked and I didn't know if I wanted to hear any more from this woman who was trying to coax me into some kind of life, and I hardened my heart against her words.

"After I put you to Fiona's breast—her being nearly crossed over with pain, you so quiet—I worked in silence cleaning her up, washing her with warm cloths, packing her with clean soft towels. In my labors I glanced up at you then and you were staring at me, watching me. Somehow we knew each other. Just then another flock of mallards flew over, returning to the waters where they were born, their summer grounds, just the way my people used to do. And yours. They remember through generations, Sophie, how to return. And then I knew. I called you the one who remembers the return."

But she never told a soul, except for Joe. He used to call me duck girl to tease me, but I never understood. So it was after the death of my babies that I got my name. And that was something to live for.

So you can see why the mallard visitation is both welcome and perhaps a portent.

Some would say that my marriage was killed by sorrow and my inability to forget and move on. Samuel certainly did, again and again. Maybe that's true, but I have often thought that perhaps marriage wasn't my lot in this life. Samuel believed I should not visit the graves, that I should live as though they were in the past. Which to me is the same as living as though they were never here at all. He did that and to his mind succeeded as long as there was enough whiskey and work. But I couldn't do that, although I was so desperate that I tried.

Even what had always been between us, the lust for each other, was dead. We could not carry on, our bodies losing their desire for each other in the fear that we would again conceive sorrow. We parted amiably and eventually his passion took another turn and he sailed back to Ulster drawn to the heroics there in a burst of Orangemen pride.

IT IS JUST PAST the summer solstice and the leaves of the birches and laurel are so thick I can only hear the notch's waters. I can tell a lot by listening, though. I can tell the mood of the air, heavy and wet or thin and light, by the sound of the river moving below. I can lie in my bed in the morning and tell you what kind of day it will likely be, if there is a storm coming. It is as if the density of the air and the wind is nature's flute, playing all the various tones and riffs of the river's voice, making a language of prophecy. When the rain is coming and the leaves are all turned backside to the air ready for a good drink, the song is a low steady hum in the background of life here at Scantic Gap.

I sit watching the antics of shiny crows come to get the stale bread I put out on the mossy boulders in the yard. Right now a squirrel and crows are in negotiation, the squirrel holding her ground, scolding. It appears one crow stops to listen, her beak full of bread, her head cocked just so, but the crows leave the squirrel to the black seed and she is triumphant. Having appeared to talk the thing over, the crows are soon back and they all eat seed together. This is what I call getting along. They, you see, are not deranged.

RAYNA AND I LIVED together peacefully for ten years. Even Angus warmed to her then and their antagonism became a game between them. Anyone could see that an almost accidental affection had developed through their shared love of me. He was grateful to Rayna, too, for helping me where he could not. My parents loved me dearly, I know that. But like Samuel, they could not abide my sorrow, encouraging me to move on. They had the sickness of forgetting, and why would I listen to them?

I learned to weave baskets from Rayna then, from split ash and sweet grass, my fingers slit and bloody much of the time. Carl, still a young man, would cut and pound out the slats for us, always using every bit that we could before stacking the remainder for the fire. And I learned to pray in a way that was so different from church prayer. Full of humility, not shame. Rayna and I sold our baskets any chance we got and soon we received orders in the mail or by word of mouth. Our little town department store was the newest thing in those days where you could get anything you wanted—that was how they sold us on the idea of it. I had to admit there was some magic in it. I would wander the aisles some days entranced by the array of goods. Anything from calico to good sharp cheese. They ordered baskets from us to hold their goods and that helped us get along. And Rayna beaded gloves and bags, a skill I never developed. She would bead all year and then take them to the Four Town Harvest fair every September where she sold them to The Ladies. We used to make fun of The Ladies, holding our pinkies out as we sipped from imaginary tea cups. But they sure loved Rayna's beadwork. She could bead anything from a bouquet of flowers to the American flag. She took in custom orders then and worked on them through the winters at the Gap.

We'd weave potato baskets and kindling baskets, log baskets. If you needed something held, we knew how to hold it. I've always loved baskets. They hold a particular magic for me. Baskets and bowls. I learned to fashion those, too. In spring Rayna and I would go down to the river, build a fire on its banks, and spend two or three days digging clay, making offerings to the spirit of the river and the earth, and shaping pots. We'd get the fire good and hot in the end and fire the pots into vessels hard as bones.

Angus and Fiona would come to help carry the pots back up the hill, insisting all the while that they didn't know why we spent such hours of labor when store-bought dishes worked faster and better. And what they didn't say, but implied—more civilized. But people had an affection for our pots. It is something peculiar in my people who emigrated here—they did everything they could to destroy the first peoples and their ways and after they were no longer seen as a threat, only then was there a looking back and a frenzy to collect and preserve their leavings. Still is. It is like a taxidermy of the soul.

There was plenty of soul left in our pots and I like to think of them still out there radiating every prayer we burned into them, collectors' items themselves now. We didn't sign them, but I'd recognize our pots anywhere, they being like children to me. The baskets, too.

So, we were busy with our baskets, pots, and beading. My autumns were spent soaking ash, readying the materials for a winter of weaving, not to mention putting up food from the garden. They still are, but less so thanks to the little bit of money that Angus and Fiona were able to leave to me, along with the by then expanded ten acres of land, three of which I rent to Carl's son who grows potatoes. I insist he grow different kinds even though the way is to grow just one. It's not safe, that. It makes the potato too vulnerable to disease. You think we would have learned from Ireland. I won't sell that land, Rayna taught me that. "Hang onto the land, Sophie, it's the only thing that has meaning and value forever." It's under my protection now but I can't control what happens to it after I die. Part of it is forested, only the three acres still for growing, and part is wetlands. There are a couple of vernal pools there, and you mustn't ever mess with them. The salamanders and toads and other beings need them for their eggs before they dry up in the summer. Remember that.

ONE SPRING MORNING I found Rayna in her bed, one of Rowena's sunrise blankets pulled up under her chin. Her right hand held a little beaded leather pouch that I knew contained the dried birth cords of all her dead children. And in her left hand, a mallard feather. That was for me, I know, to never forget who I am. I stayed in my house for a few years then, missing Rayna so. But it came time for me to move up the road, back to care for my parents in their aging years.

I was in my fifties when I returned to the Gap and I brought my babies and Rayna with me, too. I asked Rayna if could I bring her with me. And to my relief she indulged me that, came to me in a dream. Opening my hand and placing into it her thigh bone. A deliberate gesture, a soft yet fierce look into my eyes, an agreement. So, I unearthed them all, loaded them on Carl's logging truck and the beast carried them to Scantic Gap where I buried them in the side yard facing west.

And here is where I have lived alone for nearly thirty years. It is not so much that I've chosen to live alone as it's more a necessity that has chosen me. I never regretted it. In fact, I felt freer in these years than I had in my whole adult life. I still do. I can't explain it. I am lonely. Sometimes I feel as hollow of love and possibility as a dried up gourd. But there is something else, maybe that only hollow things sing. If you listen long enough you learn that, how the wind howls through the holes in the trees, the crevices between rocks. How you can play an old bone like a flute. Perhaps Rayna's naming me opened a door into the space inside me where the grief I carry and my insistence on it and on remembering had scoured me out. And when the winds of *anam*, the spirit winds entered me I was fully claimed by my name.

I am still looking for a way, you see. A way to live in this world in kinship to everything that lives in time—trees, memory, rocks, all pulsing beings, our dead. Some say it all is here now, living in different realms. Some we can see, with our eyes, some not. One must be vigilant and undistracted. Openings into the invisible world are fleet, is my belief, and I think this is where help will come from. My days are filled with a barely muted excitement of anticipation that this might be the day where another understanding might be given to me, another strand of the web reveal itself. The true web, the way the world really works.

CARL BROUGHT A LOAD of wood today. I heard the great beast of the logging truck coughing and laboring and belching up to the wood shed where he deposited large round trunks of felled trees that had grown out of the ground twisted yet strong—almost spiraled out of the earth it seems, reaching for the spare light. Carl tries to harvest only dying trees for me. He's willing to do that. He'll come back with the maul and split and stack the wood. It remains to be seen if I'll be here to use it. I stood at the window watching the trunks after he left, almost expecting them to get up and dance. It seemed to me that they hadn't forgotten how to be earthed even in their amputated state. They reminded me of the wide haunches and welcoming laps of old women squatting around the fire. I made myself a cup of tea and took it out and sat down on one of those old tree laps. There was a gentle breeze and from where I sat I could see the leaves of the quaking aspen shimmy in the wind.

My life is not my own, I realize that now. No more than a single aspen tree life is its own. Nor does my life belong to someone else, or something else, except, of course, life. I navigate this life and I am capable of running it off the rails and have come near in my young life, but I'm sure they were whispering to me, helping me move in a way that brought me through. My life never was and won't be a separate thing. I am linked, am the fruition of the dream of my ancestors, without them I would not be, and we are all the fruit of the land's dreaming, as are the deer, and the trees. My life is completely embedded in this way. I pray that I am paying my debt well and that while I am alive I plant good seeds for the future and when I die I feed the earth with my body. My life is not mine to spend any way I want, but I am a particular and unique sprouting of the dream and so aren't we all. Just think how any incalculables went into our making. How many deer, potatoes, lamb, nuts, chickens, caribou, grasses. How much loss, death, grief, love and lust. How many migrations and wanderings, how many songs, lamentations, poems and myths. How many birthings of babies, of crops, of days, of courage and despair and praise and prayers. How many wars and enslavements and dreams. And that we're here at all is astonishing—what had to befall and not befall all of us and the land in order that we live?

Do I remember how to return? No. But a name is really a thing that rides the one it owns. It is a thing to bear and to let it have its way with you, and when you do, then mysteriously you are carried by the very thing that you carry. My name has given me a good run all these many years and sometimes I feel ridden hard and put up wet. But I know that inside me there is a space where knowing of the old ways and old ones live, my bones formed around the presence of their absence. When we forget there is something real here that we cannot see with our day eyes, we're dead in the water. What I've come to see is that the remembering *is* the way of return.

If we vanish from our dead, how will they find us? If we live entirely with a mind pointed toward progress, how will the people, the land that knows us, claim us? I see that more clearly than ever now. All my life I've wanted to be known. It has taken different misguided shapes through the years but it is all rooted back to a deep and primal longing to be possessed by and to belong to land, to clan, to the wild. Yet we live in a time and in a world to which we do not belong, a world that is so far flung from itself that it seems even Isis cannot collect the dismembered pieces. I have stayed at the Gap, going round and round trying to make of my body a portal through which my dead can enter and lay claim to me. And the future, too. I am perhaps a living smoke signal, or a light flashed on a mirror. Sometimes I ask, What is the point? My heart answers, It is what's been given you.

Some things are worth standing by and if we don't find that thing in our lives, that thing given to us to stand by no matter what, no matter the fashion, the trends, we will be lost. And that is hell. Which is what we're in. A hell of our own making, at whose center we stand.

There is an old Scot story my grandfather told me of the Cailleach, the grandmother of Scotland who created the land from her apron full of stones, strewing them about. In truth she was the land herself, blue black like the stormy skies, three eyes of the past,

91

the present and the future. There were three young princes, one of whom was going to be made King. They were lost in the woods and thirsty and hungry, and one went forth in search of water and food. When he came upon a well, he threw himself gratefully upon it, marveling at the rope and bucket, when who should appear before him but a hideous old hag of a woman. He knew immediately, of course, that she was the keeper of the well and he begged a drink. Her price to him? A kiss. Well, being young and unwise, he was repulsed by her appearance and he refused, stumbling back to his brothers with the whole woeful story. Another brother bragged that he'd get water out of the old witch and off he went, but, as you can imagine, he suffered the same fate. And finally the third brother made his way to the well, and there stood the old woman and of him, too, she demanded a kiss in exchange for water from her sacred well. And this brother, he was a bit wiser knowing that a sacrifice is asked from the Holy. And he said, Of course Grandmother, and he kissed her on her lips. Whereupon she turned into a beautiful young maiden. I know you're thinking that she was under a wicked spell and through his gallantry and thirst, he broke it. And how they lived happily thereafter. I remember thinking that too, but I was missing the point of the story.

The chosen King must not rule the land, he must serve it. He must see the beauty of the land in all her guises, all her powers. He proved his willingness to do this. For the old woman Cailleach is the land and the land prevails in the end, you know. We'll all end up laid back into her, whether we're buried or go up in smoke. She's calling us into a faithfulness with her many beauties. She chooses the King.

It used to be true for all my bloods that the old women were the backbone of the community, the way mountains are the backbone of the land. As long as that was true, things would go well enough. Promises kept, rituals enacted, memory fed. But now the young and untested are held forth as hope and the way, a flimsy proposition to my mind. Now it's the ones who scale the mountain, who change the course of the river, who prevail—no longer the mountain, no longer the river, those beings of beauty and power.

As you can imagine, I refuse.

I CANNED THE BEETS today. Oh my, the glorious color of the beet juice, a dense saturated purple and yet jewel-like with the light shining through the clear jars. I splurged and lined three up on the windowsill so I could enjoy their color, even though they will spoil there. I couldn't bear to put them all in the dark. I brought some over to Rowena later in the day and when I held them up to the light, she immediately left the room, returned with an undyed skein of yarn, poured off the juice and immersed the porous wool. I laughed. Now that is living not only for survival! We sat with a cup of tea in the fading light, watching fireflies wink in and out and it made me think of my death. As soon as I mentioned it, she rose and returned with a little bottle of her best whiskey, pouring some into our tea, proper for such a talk and slapping both hands on the table, she sat, picked up her cup, and said, "You were saying?" And so we spoke about the mallards and my time coming.

"Rowena, I've thought all about it. I intend to be buried in the woods next to my relations, feeding the soil. I am praying that you and Carl will agree to break all the rules."

"You leave it to me," is what she said. And I knew I could.

"I am indebted to you and Carl," I said and we clinked our tea cups.

Sounds like a funny thing to say if I'm going to be dead, how will I pay the debt. Never mind, I will. Carl is going to gather me up and bury me in the woods in a place only he and Rowena will know, where my body can just go back to earth. I expressed my wishes that she and Carl caretake the house and land, and if in fifteen years no one has found it to be their home, the house and land will be theirs to do with as they see fit. In the meantime they can rent the house and I'll have left enough for taxes and upkeep.

The truth is, I am hoping for another looking back soul to find their way here. I am going to be working on it.

I asked Rowena then if she would weave me a blanket from that beet juice yarn, and when my time comes, wrap me in it. She reached over and squeezed my hand. I know she will. But for now, it is still the height of summer.

HOW QUICKLY THE SUMMER spent itself. The mallards flew south today over my house and I'm still here. The trees are slowly baring themselves against the sky and the leaves scuttle about in the occasional wind. There has been a windfall of acorns this year, pinging off the tin roof onto the porch. The squirrels are near delirious, as are the goats, running here and there, competing for the nutmeat. Nothing funnier than watching a goat eat an acorn, rolling it around from cheek to cheek trying to get a good purchase on the nut to crack it in two. Tonight is Halloween and tomorrow the day of the dead. I've made candied apples and a sweetened popcorn for the few kids brave enough to venture to my house. It's not that I'm all that scary, but it's pretty dark here, which can inflame the imagination. I hope so.

This morning, in the rising light, as I was busy laying out food and candles on the graves, a grey fox emerged out of the woods and into the clearing just north of the house. Not attending to me at all, she stood still, on thin fragile looking legs, her body pointed like an arrow toward the sounds of the barking dogs up the hill. One could see her deciding whether to play it cautious or bold. Decision made, not to mind, gaily flipping her head, she leapt onto the spine of the old stone wall and said, "Watch this," as she strutted nimbly down its length, like a nine-year-old girl showing off for her friends. And then she vaulted off the wall, over the clearing and onto the large boulder where yesterday I put corn out for the crows. And there she squatted and shat, just like that! And then she was gone. I laughed and laughed, so bold and sure, oh, I'd like to be like that. One could do worse than to live that way.

I SIT AT THE WINDOW with a cup of good black tea in the late afternoon. There is a gentle breeze and the steam from my tea rises and like a wraith escapes where I've cracked the window a bit to hear the geese should they fly over. The remaining yellow leaves of the black birches, barely anchored by the dark trunks and branches, appear to float like illuminated lacy islands in the dusky western sky. It's a magic trick I could delight in forever and never understand.

Tomorrow is Thanksgiving and then, soon, snow. I am taking a moment to write while bread is baking, filling the house with a scent most delicious and yeasty. Winter is a trying time here for me, alone in my little house, a life I preferred, but in winter it haunts me, my choice. If I had to say what I am terrified of it would be wandering in this human wilderness we've created, devoid of love or caring, and dying in such a state. No one to take me in. I know I am loved and have good friends in Carl and Rowena. But this fear is an old haunting, that old nightmare terror riding me, punctuated when the north wind howls around the house and my woodstove has trouble keeping things warm. Perhaps that wind raises the banshee in my blood. It is not death I fear, but the cold heartedness of people desperate to save themselves and only themselves. By the time I was born, there were hundreds of years of accumulated warfare, starvation, and uprooting running in my blood. The consequence of this, the nightmare all my people are riding, is the loss of our capacity to love beyond our own clan, and at that, it's a tight squeeze. Is survival worth such a price? To live with only survival as your guide is a mean existence, and not inevitable. Rayna taught me that. The only thing I could think that made the difference between her and my ones who came over the sea was that she never did believe that anywhere else was home except this earth. No heaven for her. She professed to be a

Christian woman—and she was, in the sense that she lived all its best ways, generosity, love—but she never gave up talking to the spirits, always in a whispering conversation with what is right here. Or *who*, really, who is right here. She made them offerings and asked for their help.

Not Angus, my old dad, he fought with the land and the elements. Every year it was a grudging match between him and storms, hail, drought, flood, and dirt. He worried and raged and cursed. It was peculiar because it was very personal, fiercely so, and yet he would never profess to a relationship with the land at all.

As you might have figured out by now, even though I am sometimes carried away by my fear, I choose Rayna's way. She made peace with her blood and peace with earth. And I'm still here doing my best to remember and to carry all my bloods, too. Because to remember is to hold on to a thread that weaves everything together. To remember is to understand where we came from, that there is a lineage. You see? This is an act of repair. We were carried long before we were born. To remind me, Rayna gave me a little white and red stone and I carry it always, sometimes in the palm of my hand, sometimes in my pocket and sometimes in my shoe but I never forget.

The latest thing they will tell you now is that not forgetting is living in the past, but some things are timeless and you have to know this. I know you think I'm old fashioned, but I know all that I need to know about current notions that say there is no real essence born into anything, not people, not the land, not anything. That all meaning is a human-made and transient thing. If nothing really means anything, what is there to live for? If that insanity catches on, it will be one of the last nails in our coffin. Yet the power of the cold and wind can undo me. Still, I have friends and will spend the Thanksgiving day with Carl's family down the road, my contribution being four loaves of fresh-baked bread and corn I blanched and froze this past summer.

WINTER NOW. This morning arrived cold and gray, even though a hot strip of fuchsia lays on the eastern horizon, foretelling sun later in the day. The white oaks and black birches, stripped to their essential winter truth, are relieved by the soft green of white pine saplings. The notch still runs on below and the trees have set their roots deeper, settling in.

Last evening, in the blue dusk, a deer came to the boulder in the yard where I lay out my little offerings, corn, seed, crumbs. I know this yearling and her mother and sibling and I worried where were they, when I saw that they lingered behind, browsing in the brush. The snow glowed white blue, the sunflower seeds black against it. I envied the boulder the deer's tongue and bristle, wishing it was my outstretched hand, wishing for such a tender trust between us. Then, the sister leapt, bounded to the boulder to share the seed, then mother. All three at the table set for their benefit. A bit later after I'd washed up the dishes, about to go upstairs for bed, I looked out again into the darker dusk where the blue had leached back to its source and the snow illuminated the last light, revealing the growth of a mysterious outcropping from the boulder. I stepped closer to the window, trying to see, and realized it was a racoon humped over the remaining seed. It amazed me that the deer had left any evidence whatsoever of their meal. But it seems to work that way, doesn't it? There is always evidence of some sort of what has transpired and the sensitive nose is the one who sniffs it out and may find a little sustenance. While I can't see them, I know her long delicate fingers, glinting eyes and razor teeth. And there waddling through the snow behind her, cuts her companion never far behind. I think they are mother and daughter.

IT IS THE TIME of the February hunger moon. I'm roasting one of Rowena's chickens and my mouth is watering. Not long ago, in this place, this was the starving time. When winter stocks were low and there might be little to eat and no way to tell when spring was coming. Sometimes I try to imagine that kind of hunger. How precious every little morsel might be in the face of death. Stone soup a feast.

Remember the arsenic. Yes, I remember what you told me. *Meat baited with arsenic intended for wolves.* Yes, I know. *They hated the wolves and they hated the people. Baiting the starving.* Yes, I'll remember. I'll scrape every little bit of meat off the bones and make a soup with them and then I'll put the bones up the hill. *Okay, then.*

We had a few inches of snow last night and Carl ran the paper up to me when he shoveled me out. He knows I always read the birth and death announcements. Being a looking back woman I keep track of who is going and who is coming. Changing places is the way I see it. The old going to where the young have just arrived from. But this morning he was all exercised about something. "Sophie you won't believe this." He ought to know there isn't much that floors me, but it's true, I'd never heard of anything like this. Anna Holmes, over on Mountain Road, is holding a funeral for a coyote. "Listen to this," he said.

Eastern Grey Coyote died on February 10th from an acute illness after suffering excruciating convulsions and suffocation. Cause of death: poison. Eastern Grey Coyote will be remembered for her exemplary mothering, having raised several litters in the woods surrounding Mountain Road, and for her haunting songs and keen survival skills. Having been displaced numerous times from her home habitat, she developed the capacity to make do without assistance. She was an avid hunter of small rodents, favoring field mice and chipmunks, but would eat carrion when need be. She displayed strength of character, curiosity and a playful humor even in the face of intense hatred. She will be dearly missed by those she leaves behind, her family pack and Anna Holmes of Mountain Road who is holding calling hours on February 12th from 9PM to midnight. All those who grieve the loss of Coyote are welcome to attend.

Poison! I looked around me for Rayna, then sat back in silence, the wind nearly knocked out of me. Carl put down the paper, grinning at the lunacy of it. If I didn't love him so much I could have smacked him. "You know what, Carl? I'm going. Some people are trying to put the world back together. You think about that."

And so tonight I fired up my old truck and drove the few miles to Anna's. The tires crunched over the snowy road which made things slow going, but gave me time to think. I've known of Anna for years, the daughter of my mother's friend Myrna, widowed young as I remember. Could it be that the coyote is somehow Anna's dead?

I parked at the bottom of the drive and a young woman with purple hair, named Maggie, gave me a lift up the hill. It was an eerie scene as we approached the fire. Firelight on the white snow, the women's faces, the dead coyote on a nearby boulder, cushioned by pine boughs. How beautiful her fur was in the light. I looked around at the women there, Anna and Emma, a woman I didn't know at all, and the young woman Maggie with two of her friends.

Anna asked if we wanted to speak a few words. I did not. I knew what had compelled me there was my bloods remembering the starvation, the arsenic, the rot. And the bear.

We were all astonished into silence when one of the women blurted out that she had poisoned the coyote. She made an anguished and tearful confession. Trying to save her remaining sheep from coyote hunger. And she was afraid and angry and grieved when she had found her most beloved ewe ripped open. I can imagine. Now she's bearing the agony of remorse for something that cannot be undone. Ever. As for forgiveness, it's not ours to give. Every living thing gets hungry. To use the tender belly of desperate need to kill a being in such a painful manner—only the deranged could think this way. There it is again. Deranged. She's got to find a way to fill the hole she left in creation is the way

I see it. Then maybe this whole grievous event will bring us closer to home.

After we buried the poor but remembered coyote, Maggie of the purple hair drove me back down the hill. I invited her for coffee some afternoon because there is something about her. I don't suspect she'll ever come, being too young to understand the invitation, but it had to be made anyway. I arrived home late and put some logs in the stove and sat down for a minute to warm my feet and have cup of tea. The tears came then.

Everything is white and blue, light radiating off ice, nearly blinding me. I stand shielding my eyes so that I can see into the distance. Something is there. Walking toward me out of the mist is the polar bear of my childhood. Escaped. We stop to consider each other, her scarred snout, her weeping yet determined eyes, me the old woman in her nightgown, weeping, too. Recognized, we move toward each other. I lay my hand on her back and we walk on together for a while.

SOMEWHERE BETWEEN the strange landscape of the dream and my little bed, I woke to the song of water.

I thought, *Am I here, or am I walking with the bear?*

All around me the world is melting. I laid there gathering me to myself, breathing in the air's prophecy of spring. Small rivers poured down the steep roof onto the tin lid of the rain barrel, making a little song. Last night the owls called late into the darkness. They'll be sitting their eggs now. The fox will be looking for mates soon, the woods filled with their wild screeching pleas. And soon the mallards will return. Maybe.

I fell in and out of the dream a few times before I could rouse myself.

Getting up to dress, I caught myself in the one mirror I own that traveled over the seas with my old ones. The glass is fading now, as am I, each chip in the gilt edges marking another year passing. I stood a long time before it, wondering who that was looking back at me. It was all a blur of smudge and features. Then I saw them emerging out of my face. As though those who haunt me had decided to reveal themselves. I don't know how I knew it was them, but I do. My once youthful face, long with high flat cheekbones, the skin white, the forehead high, blue eyes the color of corn flowers, is now flesh cockled over sharp bone, eyes retreating into the cave of their lids giving me a squinty yet alert and hawkish look. But the kindness of Rayna is there, too, a spare kindness. What has happened to my face? Are they coming for me?

I laid the fire, ate a bit of breakfast, wrapped myself in one of Rowena's blankets and sat on the porch in the sun. I laid crumbs on the railing and spoke with the sweet little nuthatches brave enough to come eat, listening, cocking their alert faces, focusing one black shiny eye that holds the whole world.

I sat here nearly the whole day, running my hands over them all—Theodore, Anna, Samuel, Fiona and Angus, Joe, Grandmother Rayna, the goaties, my old ones, their bones at the bottom of the sea and under the earth. The coyote and Anna. The bear. Thinking on my life and the life around me. Blessing every sweet and sour thing in it.

And all the time, walking with the bear.

It is one of those looking back days.

But my heart could not resist the call of spring and the afternoon sun, so I finally roused myself, put on my snow shoes and took my old self up to the woods, delighting in the slushy tracks of deer and fox speaking of other lives.

I love the way of the snow, surrendering to warmth, melting away from the tree roots making way for the new life. And the tiny fine etchings of the voles who I know will yield themselves to their fate, becoming flesh of fox or hawk. Longing to leave my tracks there, too, among them, I sat on a warmed rock, stripped off my sock and planted my old foot between deer and fox.

If the warm persists, tomorrow all three will be gone.

The Taxidermist's Daughter

You might wonder how I could, for a time, turn away from what I came to know in these rememberings I am going to tell you, but that is the danger of the life we are living, the undertow is powerful. I left home at seventeen, moved to the small city nearby and turned my back on what I knew for many years. I became sick—heart sick, home sick, bone sick, city sick, is this all there is sick. Desperate, I took to walking, like I had as a girl.

I was undone by the coyote skull.

Even in the city one can find a little pocket of sorry woods and the evidence of those who manage to survive anywhere. I found it in the leaves, probably carried off by a scavenger, picked clean and left. The light shone white on the arc of the forehead, putting the eye socket in deep shadow, a cave I fell right into, recalling another boney cave from long ago, restoring me to the self I had found, then walked away from. I had dreamed of Lou often at the edge of the woods where I had left her back then. And perhaps Louise, too.

MY NAME is Louise Estey Sewell. I was born dangling on the edge of a decade, hundreds of years after the arrival of my people to the shores of North America, and within a stone's throw of war.

After two miscarriages and one still birth, I am the only live-born child of Salome and John Sewell. On that occasion, I was given the task of fulfilling my father's one known wish. The only thing he ever wanted—a boy. My mother, remorseful about not birthing a son for my father, relinquished me to him, thus leveraging my life against her guilt.

My father was a fur and hide buyer and a taxidermist, as was his father before him and his before him. From the first moment I can remember I had been surrounded with fur. Pelts of deer, bear, raccoon and wolf had lined my bed. I never questioned it. They were a beautiful and warm comfort to me, my lap and my solace.

The pungent smell of drying hides by the woodstove and sitting beside my father as he worked became my world. When I was five years old, he gave me a my first scrap of soft deer hide on which to practice stitching. Many mornings I sat by the window, deep in concentration, making tiny stitches, the hide spotted with my blood.

It seemed that the furs and how they came to be were always an unquestioned fact of my young life. This was what my father did and I would some day do as part of a tradition. By the time I was six, I had observed the skinning of rabbits and fox, the great suspended bodies of peeled deer and caribou and bear.

I remember the mystery of the animal revealed. The molded meat and muscle, the bluish tissue that wrapped them, the open mouth, the lolling tongue. So this was dead. Is this, too, how I was made? This recognition of my own animal self sent a shiver of wonder and unease through me.

And so for the first ten years of my life, I proudly knew myself as the taxidermist's daughter. Some said it was an unseemly work for a girl. Some say that it is an unholy work, making a trophy out of a life, this work of killing and hiding the evidence in plain view. A kind of stuffed resurrection.

But it is what I knew. The daily handling of death, the quiet sitting across from my father, the only sound the inevitable buzzing of flies come to lay their future in the skins we scraped and cured.

There were two worlds there. The shop where the men gathered around the woodstove, the air blue with their smoke, their language. Some days the men were so packed into that room that they jostled the racks of guns and fishing gear, the glass cases holding the intricate and colorful fishing flies steamed with their breath, while behind the heavy canvas curtain, we sat, my father and I, skinning, stitching, shaping, mounting. Listening. We did not speak. I could not, he did not. I was nearly as mute as the death that came through our door. I alone had this in common with the dead animals that were our daily bread.

I understand now, from a distance of years, that entering into the incomprehensible world of carcass and blood and death, being dazzled by its mysteries, my speech had fled from the outside world, had become interior, until I was silent. While it was a chosen silence, it was not willful, it being an enigma to me and those around me. I found my first power there in my soul's choice not to speak. Somewhere inside myself, some part of me had begun the work that was handed to me to carry in this life. It was the first thread of the haunting, the bearing witness to the story of my people, human and animal. I listened and I watched.

Sensation and smell, the warmth of the stove, the men's voices, the pelts, the sitting and stitching, this was my life as a child. I became adept at nuance and shades of meaning, gestures, the unspoken. The shop was a murmuring and affectionate refuge from school where I was an outsider. Since I did not speak, my head was full of my own voice, and sometimes I imagined that my thoughts infused the skins that would become the death masks of deer or moose or bear.

I did not know this then, but my father's silence was not one of the calm spirit, or the deep quiet through which we can hear the unspoken. His was a silence that kills, a withholding from life, snuffing the spirit, leaving an absence where once there was an alive presence. I have come to know that silence that kills is a particularly human phenomenon. Still, our silence was a bond between my father and me, or perhaps it was the ghost of the boy I should have been that held us together, he longing for a life that was stillborn two years before me who longed to be the son he never had.

There were benefits. My father cut the most tender pieces of venison for me, and when he did talk, it was usually to me, about things that a father would speak of to a son. Or at least, this father. The fact that I was, indeed, a girl, seemed to escape his notice. He never spoke of it and from as far back as I can remember he called me Lou. Everyone did. And I tried to earn what I sensed was an elevation, a privilege.

You would think I'd have developed what they now call gender confusion, living as I did. But no, I did not, for while I was willing to take the privileges, I was clear after observing my parents that I did not want to be either of them, not man, not woman. While my mother may have struck a deal, still she tugged me wordlessly and covertly to choose who I was, which fired my father's determination to have a son and apprentice. But I had an instinct that a trap lay there in choosing one or the other and I slipped through that trap as nimbly as some foxes.

THEY SAY THAT HISTORY travels in the bloodlines, showing itself no matter our efforts to suppress the truth. Our story on this continent began three hundred years ago when my people came to the shores of Cape Cod, seeking to create a New Jerusalem where they could purify themselves and their church. Escaping from a polluted and corrupt England, they brought with them their god of fierce retribution and their devil who flies through the air looking for a willing body to do his work. Indeed the devil was everywhere, even in my pious way-back maternal grandmother, Mary Estey, who was accused and hung as a witch, having been condemned to death by my way-back paternal grandfather Sewell.

My parents lived out that distant lineage in their lives. My taciturn father walked a straight and narrow path, his silent disapproval an attempt to restrain my mother's wildness, while she veered as far away from capture as possible. Always slipping the noose.

My father had a fine eye for recreating wildlife, for the detail of ears cocked to hear the predator approach, to the ripple of tongue, and yet he had little understanding of life itself. Or so it seems to me. Blindly ridden by history, he was unaware of the voices of the dead speaking through his actions, his own and those he held in his hands every day. His refusal to hear them was a lock on his heart.

He seemed to think that god had it in for him, his marriage to my mother being part of the evidence. And yet I have come to believe that while they quarreled often, they needed each other in the deepest way. Circling like two halves of something that could not live without the other, like predator and prey, the chase strengthening both. His reticence and disapproval fired her passions, in turn justifying his efforts to control the wildfire, which gave him a kind of cold and focused passion of his own. They reminded me at times of a fox with a mouse, entrapping, pouncing. Although who was the fox and who was the mouse on any given day owed itself to some invisible lottery I could not discern. Sparks flew between them, making for a cold warmth.

MY MOTHER, Salome Estey Sewell, was a Puritan Queen. Beautiful and elegant, she had that particular pride that I imagine only the righteous could carry, along with an electric vitality of rebellion against that same righteousness.

Her soul being one gifted with a fine yet wildish sense of beauty and a love of the mystical, she believed in signs and wonders. One night I dreamed her dancing naked except for a fine winter doe skin, stepping high and proud as I had seen the deer step alert and wary. She had a certain scent, my mother did, a heated scent that perfumed her skin and reminded me of the pelts I slept among. She was named for the one who danced for Herod in order to gain the head of John the Baptist. What kind of dance, I wondered, when I encountered that passage in my Bible studies, flushing at the recognition of this ancient Salome in my dream.

109

That Salome of old, fusing with my mother in my mind, smoldered in my imagination, and I wondered at such a courageous but immodest name given to a woman whose ancestors forbade dancing.

My mother did radiate a kind of heat, my father cold. I could always tell when they would come together, the air moving differently, restless, pacing, hissing. It is fitting that this woman whose namesake courted such danger should marry my father, for how dangerous it must be to daily handle the dead. I imagine his blood encrusted fingers on her breasts, her musty scent overcoming his restraint, releasing his lust for which he would hate himself on those mornings when the sizzle had been spent leaving a tender yet wretched fog of musk issuing from their bedroom. I knew he would be especially restrained on those days, while my mother would ride an invisible energy, robust and full.

The building that housed their shops sat on our Main Street, shaded by large Dutch elms planted by my ancestors. My father's shop occupied the right side of the one story clapboard building, my mother's the left. John Sewell's Taxidermy, one thin wall away from Salome's Lingerie and Corset Shop. Gun racks shared a wall with women's undergarments, fashioned by Salome from imported French lace and silk, canvas and cotton, with stays of bone from whale and moose.

Her gift as a lingerie maker was much admired by the women who patronized her shop. She was known as a woman with a wicked ability to know just the right lingerie that was called for to home an errant husband. At least temporarily.

My parents were both in the business of longing. My mother catered to the women who brought to her their tender longing to believe that it was possible to revive their youth and to conjure the boys they had married. They wanted to believe that the loud voice issuing through the wall of my father's shop was not the voice of the boy they had married, whom they wanted to resurrect, to seduce into return, a magic trick of the gods.

110

My mother let them think that it was possible, although I knew she knew better. What was the harm in fostering the illusion that a piece of frill and a tiny waist was power? Maybe more than she had bargained for.

So, the women patronized my mother's shop, the men my father's. It not being unusual for me to stuff his kill in the morning and to corset her body in the afternoon, both mounted for display, restrained within the forms of our artistry. The only difference being one still had a choice. Or did she?

Even though I had been claimed early on by my father—his Lou—both my parents saw that I was gifted with a needle and had a good eye for translating the image into the form. So while on most days I sat with my father, innocently apprenticed to and loving a craft that served his ancestral project of taming what both compelled and frightened him, the wild and those who lived in it, my mother recruited me often to work intricate pieces. Many afternoons found me, having washed, in her words, *the stench* from my hands, sitting on her turquoise couch in the sunny and feminine back room of her shop, and sewing.

While my father and I did not speak, my mother talked, perhaps to make up for our silence, and while I appeared not to, I listened. It was as if there was always a small party going on there, a little nerve center of the town, women carrying stories of hard and bloody labors, hard and bloody deaths. Cracked nipples, painful monthlies, and cold beds. They made sly and bawdy jokes about the marriage bed, and who was in it and who was out of it. Who was getting it and who was not. They wept for what they had lost, the men who lay beside them at night, spirited off by a war they could not speak of, the mysteries of it, hidden from them, unutterable.

Most afternoons I came straight from school to sit among what men were there on any given afternoon, the third shift, the tradesmen, the guys who were unemployed and some unemployable, too broken by a war that chased them still. The men greeted me warmly, if awkwardly, when I came through the door to sit among them, having a small snack before I went to work for my father. There was the usual, "Hey, Lou, how was school today? Learn anything good?" to which I smiled and shook my head, and after a slight and awkward silence they would pick up their talk, their voices mild in my presence and rough with smoke. Those men smelled of aftershave and whiskey and tobacco and, in those moments, I felt safe. In those moments, I loved them in my way.

The men talked as though my silence rendered me invisible. And that was okay, that's why I knew everything about them, even what they had not revealed. There is some advantage in this, as I learned to love them in spite of themselves, and in spite of how I came to hate them with a passion that seared the walls of that shop. But there was always a part of me saved back and on guard. While the lives of the men who gathered around the fire, who stamped through the door smelling like woods and tobacco, the fresh air and cold clinging to them, called to me, I could imagine such a life, but it was not allowed to me as a female. And I couldn't really be a boy.

While I rode the prongs of that dilemma, it was clear to me that in some deep way the men both needed and resented the women. They would complain sometimes, having their smokes, when there was a lull in hunting stories, about their bosses, how they were being screwed, about the haves, they being have-nots. It only took one to get the other men thinking. This didn't bother me much, but when the complaining came round to their wives, I was worried because I had seen in my mother's shop the results of those sessions, the black eyes, the bruised arms.

And so I spent the early years of my life trying not to be the worst insult the men could hurl at each other after a two-beer Saturday afternoon story swap around the woodstove—a *pussy*. I heard it many times, Oh, you pussy. Even though I knew they flung it at each other in good nature, I knew it was something not to be and that it had something to do with being female and since

I was born into a woman's body, that included me, unless, of course, I joined them against a part of my self. And I wasn't going to do that, never. So, over time I decided I would simply be myself in a girl's body, trying to avoid all the trappings of both as best I could.

I came to see that they talked on and on to distract themselves from the knowledge of what they had done, what was done to them and what they grieved, in the war, in the woods, and in their homes. They didn't know it, but we were where they came for a kind of absolution. *That* was our art, to turn their failings into trophies.

And those men, they seemed to me to be as stalked and trapped as the animals they hunted. They were, most all of them, veterans of the world war that had ended a few years before I was born and now they worked at the local defense plant, a huge city sprawling over several blocks devoted to the defense of one people and the destruction of another is how I came to see it. But they were both proud and restless in a work that demanded so little of them. And so much.

All day long they assembled tiny parts, passing them on to the next person who assembled another tiny part. Never part of the whole, it made sense to me that this would transfer into a life, a life of parts. A certain insanity. While they told themselves this life was certainty after the uncertain times of war, they itched for the same depth of purpose they had experienced fighting evil.

They killed for meat, but not only for meat, otherwise my father and his father and his would not have thrived on the business of taxidermy. Otherwise they would not pay us to make trophies to hang above their fireplaces in their new post-war ranch houses. Taught to hunt by skilled hunters—fathers and grandfathers who killed for necessity—they hunted to remember who they were before they were asked to forget. They hunted to provide what was no longer needed in a world turning to slaughterhouses and grocery stores. They hunted and killed to remember and to overcome the wild in themselves, a wild that had no home in their assembly-line lives and found its expression in terrifying ways. They were providers who had become collectors, trying to feed an insatiable longing for a dignity that they felt was forever lost to them.

Those men were on fire for what they had lost, the long, slow fuse of longing singeing them from the inside, smoldering in their blood, becoming a dangerous demand for possession.

Their invisible desires took on muscle in that shop, an alive unspoken force, it being my father's work to confirm them in their want and in the illusion of its rightness and its fulfillment. And to this I was apprenticed.

AS THE YEARS WENT BY I learned to scrape and work the hides of small animals—rabbit, raccoon, skunk. I'd watch my father carefully remove the skin, skillfully cutting around the eyes, the mouth, the ears, gently pulling the skin off the tail like removing a woman's nylon stocking.

I stood beside my father, each of us at our respective fleshing beams, mine a miniature of his, removing the fat and tissue and fur with bone handled crescent fleshing knives, learning not to tear the tender skin of the yearling. We moved back and forth over the beam in a kind of genuflection, scraping the hides under the arc of the blue sky and deep colors of autumn, companions in silence. In the early years, my father brain-tanned each hide and we were strong and brown from our hard work. Any discomfort that I had, any questions about the animals themselves, I put into the hands of my father, unspoken, trusting myself to what I thought was his greater wisdom.

UNTIL MY TENTH BIRTHDAY life went along that way. On that morning I scuffed down the short block through the dead leaves at my feet. Fall was early that year, gold lay and continued to fall all around me, the yellow black birch leaves landing on the mossy graves whose inscriptions were almost gone back to earth, they were so old. I carried a stick, running it along the wrought iron fence, clanging out a happy birthday to myself and thinking about what it meant to be born.

It was hunting season and the shop was already busy, cars parked in the small lot facing Main Street. On one roof, a doe was lashed, her neck curving back exposing her tender throat. I stopped to run my hand along that soft place, almost still warm, before I entered the shop where my father greeted me, "Happy birthday Lou," the men on cue singing "Happy Birthday" to me in harmony. So unlike him, my excited father took me into the workshop where he handed me a small package wrapped in newspaper and butcher's string. Inside, a sturdy leather sheath held my own pearl-handled skinning knife. "It is time," he said, " for you to try your own hand," and he lead me to the work bench where a cottontail rabbit lay in a soft crumble of death.

I could hear the wind picking up, dried leaves clattered against the door, the creak of the flagpole across the street at the general store. My father's breath blew warm puffs against my face as he leaned down to me in anticipation of my gratitude. "Bud snared it this morning. He said it had your name written all over it, Louise, because its your birthday. "

Louise. My name startled and flew between us then, or perhaps let go with a great recoil. Like in tug of war when you've been holding on to the rope so long and suddenly the other side, admitting defeat, gives way and sends you sprawling onto the ground, gasping for wind. I had not known, until that moment, that some part of me had been in a silent war.

When he said my name—Louise—my own name entered into me, cracking open the possibility of my own world, releasing me from an old agreement I had not known I was bound to.

Maybe like many tortured men, my father was knowledgeable in the ways of servitude. He knew how to bind me to him, a little smile here, a word of approval there, parsed out to me so skillfully

115

that I craved more, I became enslaved to the project of satisfying him, imagining the pleasure that would flood me under the full glow of his approval. Because he was so sober, I longed for his sun to rise on me and because of me, and he held out that promise. My father thought I was tractable. And I was. He had come to rely on my obedience, what he thought of as my malleable nature that both served him well yet was contemptible in a girl who should have been a boy.

It could have gone on that way. I shudder to think how long, still maybe, even though he is long dead, if he had not called me Louise on that day. That slip was his confession, and a betrayal of everything I had harnessed my life to up till then. Being his Lou. The cage had opened, but did I want to take my freedom?

He knew what he had done. And if he could, he would have unwound that moment, would have swallowed that "Louise." And he tried.

There was a turmoil in my blood, I was confused, I looked from him to the rabbit. I hesitated, trying to absorb what had just happened. And in an effort to gain back what he knew somewhere he had by his own voice released, he pounced, "Don't be a pussy, Lou."

So I took that rabbit on my lap, took up the knife and skinned the soft body. All the while a litany running through my thoughts, *Louise* skins this rabbit, *Louise* is skinning this rabbit, on her tenth birthday, *Louise* skinned her first rabbit, over and over. I carefully peeled away that skin, and a part of Lou, too. But it would be a secret, even from me, the same way I had always been careful to mask from the both of us what my father would assume was a weakness of girlish feeling, the ripple of sympathy that moved under my skin when the hide was cut and pulled down around the bluish body of meat and muscle.

It was clear on that day that I had a particular and careful skill that put a gleam of pride in my father's eye. I remember still his taking that skin out into the front room to show the men gathered there what his Lou could do.

And someone inside my mind said, *Lou is dying.*

MY MOTHER SENSED the rift between me and my father. She had waited for the proper moment to reclaim her daughter. I see that now. She had given me to my father hoping it would be what would unlock his heart and give him to her. Knowing it was a mistake and regretting it almost from the moment she agreed to this unholy bargain, she waited. She knew Louise had come between my father and me on that day, fraying our bond if not yet severing us. She knew it the way an animal knows, smelling it, her whiskers vibrating with portent, and she took the opening.

On the afternoon of that very long day, the day when Lou began dying, I sat on my mother's turquoise and quilted silk couch. Bought in a wild push against what she saw as the drab prescriptions of a proper life, it presided like a queen in the back room of her shop. She had asked me to come in order to work on a particularly complicated and frilly corset for her friend, Roxie, a woman who, because she had separated from her husband, was of a questionable reputation in our small town. Even though no one could blame her, they held her in suspicion nonetheless. She'd been married to Bud, the man who that morning had killed the rabbit for my birthday. While she had left him, he had not left her, showing up at my dad's shop when he knew Roxie would be with my mother.

I didn't like Bud—more than once I'd seen the bruises on her arms, once a blackened eye. Yet he was often kind to me, and I reconciled that confusion by widening the difference between Roxie and me. I had earned his kindness, she his rage. It was as though she and I were different species of female, me tough, her weak. Her courage in leaving him was not lost on me, though. I knew how people speak of such women.

117

They sat, my mother and Roxie at the little round table, a Wedgewood blue teapot and two dainty cups on their gold rimmed saucers laid out between them, the steam rising up into air. My mother brought me a cup of tea, put it beside me on a small table.

I was happy to sit and sew and think about what had happened that morning, about Lou and Louise, trying to sort out my feelings. My mother thought she could slip it past me, my eyes being focused on the tiny stitches, but I saw her through the veil of my hair as she took a little amber bottle from her notions bag and poured a medicinal drop or two into Roxie's and then her cup along with the Oolong tea. I was shocked but interested.

As the tea worked its way into me and the amber into Roxie and my mother, a kind of peace infused the room. With the autumn light and wild wind swirling around the building and the women's voices murmuring, I fell into the trance of handwork. When I next looked up to take a sip of tea, my cup was gone, secreted away in my reverie. At the table, my mother and Roxie huddled close, holding the teacup in their hands between them, staring intently into its depths. Lowering my hands to my lap, curious, I watched and waited. Without looking up, my mother said, "We're reading the leaves of your tea, Lou. Trying to see what the future brings. After all, it's your birthday."

And I thought, whose future? Lou's? Louise's? When she saw my consternation, my mother laughed, trying to make light. "It's something my mother used to do, and hers. Probably nothing." But I could tell that what she saw made her pensive.

"Maybe you should tell her, Salome."

I cut her a look that said, Tell me what?

The bells on the shop door tinkled then and Roxie stood up, straightened and smoothed her skirt, checked the seam in her stockings, and with her thumb and index finger she cleared the lipstick at the corners of her red mouth the way she had a habit of doing. "I'll handle it Salome," she said, and wobbled out to the sales room.

Never taking my eyes from my mother, I waited. The way I'd seen animals wait to see what you were going to do, were you friend or foe. The afternoon sun streamed in through the sheer lace curtains and onto the turquoise couch, warming me. Roxie's cigarette smoke lingered and curled up and around my mother like a blue spirit.

That's when my mother brought up Mary Estey, her great grandmother who was hung. She had spoken of her before and it seemed like ancient history and I wondered what it had to do with me now. "History doesn't lie flat, Lou," that's what she said to me, then rushed on to say, "and when you were born on the same date that she was hung, I wondered if that was an omen, if that wasn't history speaking to us somehow. Your father thought I was crazy but I thought you're old enough to know and you should." She stopped abruptly and her words hung in the air between us. When I didn't respond, she rushed on. "She was a strong woman who spoke out in her own defense, a dangerous thing for a woman to do. You remember, that you have that in your blood. Just be careful." Of what, I wondered.

If this had been the day before, Lou would disdain it, would declare that this history had nothing to do with her, just another story about a woman who was a victim and so long ago. And the coincidence, just that. But the words kept running through my mind, *Lou is dying.*

And Louise? If she accepted this story as having to do with her, she would have to join this tribe of females who were so confusing and so powerful and yet so bruised and loyal. They could make men need them, but could not defend themselves against their fists. Not unlike the deer, I thought, whom the men longed for, sat hours in wait of, told stories about that brought tears to their eyes, but who were powerless to protect themselves in the face of this dangerous longing.

It was as if in those few moments my mother and I were lifted out of time, encapsulated in that room with the smoke and

119

the steam from the tea, her perfume. The wind mimicked the creak of the gallows as the rope swung under Mary's weight, the soft cries of her family, while next to her hung the peeled body of the rabbit I had skinned so skillfully just that morning, their blue tongues protruding and swollen.

Bud's loud voice broke the trance.

"Come on, Ro, I promise I'll never do it again, may god strike me dead if I ever lay a hand on my Ro again. Come home, baby," his voice both pleading and knife-edge dangerous. My mother moved quickly, laying a hand briefly on my shoulder before rushing into the shop where Bud was arcing out his right fist about to bring it down on Roxie' head. They'd rehearsed this many times, he threatening, she cowering. But she had forgotten her part, and instead in one motion kneed him in his balls, grabbing the scissors off the counter as he crouched in pain.

"God doesn't have anything to do with this, Bud. You come near me again and I'll cut them off, I swear, and feed them to the next fox you trap."

When he raised his head, ready to rise up and charge, I was there. Maybe it was his own self he saw in the eyes of a ten year-old girl. I don't know. But it scared him.

He smiled. "Happy Birthday, Lou."

As I stood looking at him, in a flash his affection turned mean. I could sense that. Yet I knew he'd have my father to answer to if he ever laid a hand on me. The irony of the moment was not lost on my young self, the precarious balance of needing protection from the one you need protection from, but still I held fast.

The tension nearly broke the beams of sunlight that came to pool on the oak floor between us, illuminating Bud's face with an otherworldly light, obliterating time.

I knew I was going to speak then, had to.

"Even if you kill her, you can't have her," I whispered.

Having never heard me utter a word, Bud looked at me stunned, momentarily off guard, but quickly sized me up for the snare.

"Yeah, Lou, but nobody else will either. She's mine. You're too young. It's none of your business."

My father's words came back to me, *Bud snared it for you, Louise, he said it had your name written all over it.*

"Is your name written all over Roxie?"

I really wanted to know.

But before he could lunge or answer me, the door behind him burst open and the men from next door took him away. Silent, my mother and Roxie returned to the back room and the little amber bottle. Forgotten, I stood in that little pool of light, soaking in the warmth, wondering whose name was written all over me.

BESIDES THE RIVER, the library was my refuge and I needed it now. I skipped school the next day and went there, inwardly daring my mother to challenge me. But when it came to breaking rules, Salome almost always went in favor of small rebellions. My father was another matter, and I conspired with my mother on that day not to tell him.

I loved our tiny round library that always smelled of paper and glue and in winter of wet wool. It was a warmish day and the librarian had cracked open the windows on the south side to let in the air and the songs of crickets. I went to the little card file, thumbing through looking for the Salem trials. I never accepted the librarian's help. I preferred tracking things down by myself. And that way she could not determine for me if what I wanted to know about was fitting for my age. I hated that. The chair squealed on the linoleum floor as I drew it close to the open window.

I read about the Puritans and understood that Mary Estey, while innocent, was killed by the execution of her belief that the devil travels through the air and can enter into a person. And I considered the truth of that, for hadn't I seen something possessing Bud?

It was not lost on me, this thing about familiars, a witch's animal companion who did her bidding. There was some hidden story here between women and animals and men—mysterious and dangerous, unspoken and scary. I had felt it in both shops, I had heard it from both the men and women, I had seen it in bruises and sensed it in the animals I held under my hands.

It was all confusing, and while I often put it away from my mind, it shadowed me, demanding that I engage with it, and I tried to because they were my questions that had emerged with Louise and I would make a place for her, a place kept secret, even a little bit, from me.

My father continued to call me Lou and I continued to be a good and obedient son, all the while the coals of Louise smoldered. While Lou had always floated in the field of the stories, now Louise both stood back and entered into them at the same time, trying to understand. I sometimes imagined her, while my head was bent to close work, with a knife in her teeth, diving deep into that confusing adult world where shadows lurked and doubled back on themselves like underwater grasses that could trap and pull us under. I wanted her to use her knife to cut through the complications, the entanglements of love and attachment, longing and its delusions, in order to see clearly.

Louise and Lou were trying to sort out their alliances, it is clear to me now, but then it was a muddle. Who was Lou? Who was Louise?

BEHIND THE SHOPS there was a large meadow bordered on three sides by woods. In the winter the snow covered fields stretched out from behind the store like a flat white sheet. The snow was an alive thing, just waiting for the animating breath of wind to send it flying in waves, rolling, airborne, like when we changed the sheets and billowed them before securing them taut and still again.

I was alone in the store on that day, a Sunday, doing hand work on a pair of doeskin gloves lined with the fur of a rabbit. I had turned twelve that fall and had just shown my first blood, a friend, according to my mother, a curse according to the girls at school who seemed oddly excited to speak of this curse. Maybe it was because my mother was done with childbearing and every month held her breath awaiting her friend to show up, birth control being illegal still. As for the girls, to speak of it as a curse was to enter a club through some kind of painful initiation. All I know is that I felt funny. A nervous restlessness of the unknown. So I welcomed the chance to be alone, to sit accompanied by the metallic voice of the woodstove as I alternately stitched and looked up to dream with the wind, to look out through curtainless windows on what might be to some a desolation, and was to me, too, except that my mind could breathe there, with only the sound of the fire, the air, the tick of the clock, the occasional whistle of wind herding the snow before itself.

At the edge of the clearing where the meadow meets the woods, my father had built a square, fenced-in area of wood and chicken wire. He built it several feet into the earth, deep and tall enough to discourage scavengers, except for the chickadees and nuthatches who dined on the fat, an occasional turkey vulture, and the crows, of course. This is where he brought the remains of the animals he had skinned and butchered. He called it the dump, but I secretly thought of it as the bone cage.

I have come to see it as god's workshop where sculptors named beetle and worm and bacteria, crow, chickadee, and vulture, diligently, even lustily, transformed the raw and bloody corpses of the animals we had skinned into the arc and planes of scapula and pelvis, bowls of skulls. Nothing was wasted in the seething cauldron of the bone cage.

He had made a trip down the day before, carrying a fox carcass. I could still see his snowshoe tracks not yet covered by the windswept snow.

When I saw movement down at the cage, I picked up the binoculars my father kept on the bench. I stood at the window then, not breathing, as I watched a fox slink cautiously up to the cage, pausing every few feet to look around. It was red against the snow, alive and furred, so unlike the revealed and vulnerable one that lay there. When it reached the body of the skinned fox, separated only by chicken wire, I could see it set up a call of some sort. I watched as it alternately tried to stick its paw through the wire and then grip it with its teeth, giving up to sit in what I can only call a forlorn fashion, laying down finally, head on front paws, like a dog, I thought.

Dusk dropped a veil over the distance, and I watched that fox until I couldn't see it anymore, my chest constricted, breath held, only the sounds of the old building and the wind and the clock. The trickle of blood oozing onto the pad between my legs, the tears tracking down my face.

There can be such a fine line between innocence and knowing, and I crossed it on that day. The crossing took place in my heart, not yet in my mind. I did not understand why or what had happened really, except that I had felt some kind of movement inside me, a quickening in my belly I would come to know as regret.

I left the shop that night, bundled in my winter coat, its fox collar up around my cheeks, keeping me warm. I walked the long way home, past the graveyard where my grandparents were buried, the school, the convent where the nuns floated along the sidewalk after leaving evening mass at the church next door. They disappeared into their house like the birds in the old cuckoo clock my mother wound every morning. I half expected them to emerge again and waited a bit, but when they did not, I went on.

As I walked and the fur riffled around my face, I thought about the fox I had seen in what looked like a posture of mourning that made my heart ache. Could it be that the fox had feelings and loved similar to me? I thought then about my father's silence and wondered, was it guilt? Maybe remorse. Was mine? I wondered if that was the shadow over his heart that he could not name. I walked down through the hollow where mist was rising off the river, telling us a warm front was coming in, a January thaw in February.

By the time I reached home I had a made a decision that even though I knew *something* had happened and even though I did not know exactly what had taken place by the bone cage, or in me, I knew it was not something to tell. And I did not.

The door that had cracked open on my tenth birthday—when my father called me Louise, when I had hesitated to skin the rabbit, when my mother told me of Mary Estey, when Bud's name was written all over Roxie—swung wider now. Beyond the threshold I sensed a mournful story assembling itself, one I did not want to look at, one that would exile me from the story I had lived by.

I was nauseous and dizzy, spending the next day in bed, telling my mother that it was cramps. I dozed fitfully all day, getting up to wander from window to window, thinking about the fox, thinking about Lou and Louise as the fog rose up from the snow, shrouding the yard and the old stones in the graveyard next door.

In the early evening I sank into a dream of a small one-room cabin filled with a suffused golden lamplight, where fox, deer, and bear pelts draped over my bed. It was home and breathed a sense of comfort and safety, a refuge from the harsh world. Then I saw Lou, her body splayed in front of the door, dead and naked, a bloody hole where her heart had been. Horrified, my own heart slamming in my ribs as I ran to leave the cabin, stopping when I saw that I would have to step over Lou's dead body. As if by an unseen hand, the door swung open and there before me stood a bear, a deer, and a fox. Peeled and bloody.

Unmoving, they gazed at me with neither recrimination nor love, neither absolution nor forgiveness but something more frightening. Knowing.

I saw that in the fox's muzzle she held Lou's heart. They moved toward me, then by me, entering the cabin where they reclaimed their skins. Returning to the threshold, they faced me while my blood pounded, beating out a rhythm, *Run! Run!*

We stood there between one life and another, suspended in time, the long distance of evolution between us. In their gaze, I remembered then all the things that we are, that all those who have carried us to this time are still here, alive in us, rising up in our dreams to claim that relation, to remind, to restore. Did they see my remembering?

They stood taking the measure of that girl who had learned to wield the knife and whose misguided love of them could not sustain them. They turned then and stepped over Lou, dead on the threshold, and off into the woods beyond, but for the fox who stood facing me still, Lou's heart in her mouth. Her bright eyes pierced the tough muscle of my heart—her gaze an arrow of pity and keen exactness. She bent then and returned the heart to Lou's body, who stood and turned to me, her eyes glinting like the fox, before she turned away and they walked off toward the forest together.

I stood watching them until they turned one last time before disappearing into the sedge.

I woke in the deep of night with a start. Bereft, bereft. Awash in the sick remorse of knowing that my father and I were wrong, my fingers worried the fur beneath them. I knew that I was not absolved of wielding the knife, but spared nonetheless, both a merciful reprieve and a torture.

I lay awake yet moving in and out of the dream. It is just a dream, I told myself. I am crazy to put stock in a dream. But I could not shake the realness of it, the world of the dream.

The thought rose up then, what if the dream *is* a world. The meeting there on that threshold was as real as any meeting in waking life. And what I saw there on that threshold, their eyes entering me, was a story of intelligence I could not refuse.

You're crazy, I heard my father's voice, and his father's, and his.

I was afraid. What if I was deranged?

I laid out two paths, one if I was crazy, one if I was not.

The first frightened me more, for if I was crazy, where would I go for help? A terrible loneliness threatened to engulf me.

And yet, if I was deranged, I would not be accountable for my actions, would I?

But when I imagined ignoring the dream and the fox at the bone cage, when I imagined walking the path of not crazy, I felt sickened at the thought of having to continue to do my father's work as before, as though nothing had changed when everything, somehow, had.

Louise, you saw the fox at the cage. There was another voice inside me now, and an almost unbearable tension rose up in me as I saw myself straddling the threshold where the dead body of Lou had been. What was I to trust, the dream or my people?

Choose.

My mother called me then to go down to the shop. I watched myself get up and dress while my mind stripped down to a hard truth—I was born into a seething conspiracy of conflicting loves and hates, of silence and cruelty between men and women, between human and animal. The animals were the sacrificial lambs at the altars of a cruel and distorted world. And the dead and good girl on the threshold, too.

I was not ready to know this. I wanted life to stand still while I figured it out. I wanted life to be one thing, predictable. I wanted people to behave in a way that I could trust and to grow up knowing who I was and how I fit in.

Choose.

I took the long way round to my father's shop. The trees cracked with cold while my mind was hot with a growing rage thinking about the dead girl and how trusting I had been. And my heart filled with sorrow knowing what I had done. By the time I

127

arrived at the shop, from out of the fuels of love and rage that could make the courage I needed to live in their world, I had chosen rage.

I had chosen to trust the dream. I had chosen to trust what I felt in my own flesh. I would follow the one they would say is crazy. I could not go back. I would be at odds with my people, but not myself. Not with Lou, not Louise. And not the animals.

By the time I reached the shop I was flooded with a torrent of righteous anger that carried me through the narrows of a lifelong fear and into the dangerous and liberating waters of will. I was a building storm front, just waiting to spend her wrath.

My father stood at the workbench, leaning on his forearms, thinking about what was next to do.

"Jesus, you're late, Lou. Where you been?"

I said nothing, sat at my usual stool to his right and picked up my knife, hefting it in my palm, feeling the moral weight of the gift he had given me.

"What's the matter with you, Lou," he said, leaning over the bench to pick up the limp body of a fox and toss it casually onto the bench in front of me. "Still on the rag?"

I was lightning quick with all the speed and alert wariness of the fox. I lunged, saying over and over "No, no, no, NO!" as I looked into his frightened and uncomprehending eyes and clenched my hand on his forearm, holding it to the bench. And I could see that when I put my hand on his arm he took it for a gesture of reconciliation even in the midst of my rebellion. I could see him deciding how to use this betrayal, whether or not to be merciful with Lou, how to milk my treasonous moment, when suddenly I drove the knife through, hissing, *"My name is Louise."*

A trance of wilfulness came gushing through me, exhilarating me with my own power to determine the next moment as years of silence, years of being a good and naked and dead girl on the threshold of my father's life coursed through me and I was free to determine my name.

Anguished, he yelled, "Louise!" delivering us from my violence into an otherworldly and soundless place. A timeless place. We stood stunned and staring at his bleeding hand, next to the dead fox, and my father, seeing that his blood stained the fur, spoke.

"Move the fox," he said, his voice flat and cold.

And I, incredulous at what I had done, incredulous that my father would, with his hand crucified to the bench, still think of the pelt of the fox, moved her. *Her, I moved her.* Our eyes locked as he pulled the knife from the wood and then his hand. To my astonishment I saw that beneath his puzzled hurt, he was relieved.

I could see the letting down, the dissolving of any illusions he had clung to against his own wretchedness. I was the final betrayal, his beloved Lou, his hope that perhaps there was some good in him, that god had finally blessed him, that he somehow deserved this love, this obedience he misunderstood for love.

His relief was fleeting. I knew he had already weighed the future and that while now he could sink into his miserable fate, the love for me that had energized him now turned to the fuel of hate. I had become the predator and he the prey as surely as if I had turned on him and bitten him. He would not question his complicity in my act. He was not a reasonable man, but ran on a kind of numb emotion and self pity and now I was his legitimate enemy. And yet, I was still his child and whether or not loving me as a son was fair to me, love me he had, and he knew it was the proper way.

All this calculation went into those few seconds when our eyes locked. Then we heard my mother knocking on the door that adjoined the shops. We looked at the door and then each other, a secret agreement not to speak of what had happened passing between us. An agreement to keep her out of our hate as we had kept her out of our love. An agreement so tangled with everything that had arisen for both of us that I am sure if asked we could not speak our reasons.

My mother never entered my father's shop unless she had to. But when we didn't answer she turned the knob and stepped through into our scene of blood, the air so thick with enmity and conspiracy it was a wall that stopped her, frozen.

"What on earth, John?"

"An accident, Salome. I was teaching Lou and the knife slipped," reaching for a clean rag under the bench to wrap his hand, speaking quickly, me frozen to the spot, watching my mother, caught somehow, but in what? My father was saving face in front of her. I knew that. And for the first time in my life, I pitied him. I was no fool. I understood that the pitied can be merciless in their humiliation and so I was wary. But again he implicated me in this deception. Did I want rescue from him, or from her?

Louise reached toward my mother and Lou stood her ground. Who *was* I?

WHEN I STABBED MY FATHER on that day, it was the barest surfacing of the lifelong subterranean roiling inside of me. To my mind, when he threw the fox like so much trash, my father's hand enacted the crimes of his mind, just as his ancestor had enacted the crimes of his belief when he hung my grandmother.

But there is also this: I had, for the moment, traded places with him. I had pinned him as he had pinned me so many years before, to an identity that was not mine, to an unholy alliance that denied who I was. My mother had committed this crime as well, but the real damning thing now was that I had learned at his knee how to see the animals as much a possession as he saw me. But what could I do? I had no place to go. I knew that I should love my father, but my pity would have to be my love. I could no longer afford any more than that.

We tacitly agreed in that moment not to speak of it, to bury it, to go on. For all the blood, his wound was not serious, luckily. The point was made though, in blood, to both of us. His hand

130

healed and we resumed our lives, me sitting across from him, working the skins, to all appearances, as I was taught. But what was buried between us, pulsed from the earth like loosed uranium, seemingly inert yet dangerous. And what had loosed in me?

There was one difference. From that moment on, he called me Louise.

IT WAS THE FIRST tender arrival of spring, and in a few months I would be fourteen years old. It had been a little over a year since the winter I stabbed my father and I spoke now, yet rarely, to people. I introduced myself to the trees, to the fox, to the river—to whoever was listening to me. *My name is Louise.* To the something I could feel but not see. I had taken up walking in every spare moment, down by the Scantic river, up through the meadows across the pastures and the surrounding woods where the men hunted. I was looking for Lou and the animal heart she carried.

I walked along the river, the dark river, along a deer path that is cut there, traveled for perhaps hundreds of years. I placed my feet one after the other alongside the rushing cold water, not able to keep up, being weighted by bone and flesh and all the stories that lived inside of me, all the human frailties of generations I unknowingly was trying to sort out. The water carried its own stories of time and place, yet seemed to carry them so much lighter than I did mine, moving around what rose up to meet it with a presence I was trying to find.

There was a brew cooking inside of me of confusion and hatred, love and remorse. Remorse about what I had done, what I continued to participate in, hatred of my father who enlisted me in his distorted view of the world, and of my mother for tacitly agreeing. I hated the men who came into the shop with their swaggering stories, and I disdained them because I felt sorry for them, as trapped as the animals they hunted. And I hated the women, with a skill learned at my father's knee, for their whining, their tears and, most of all, their vulnerability at the hands of the men they loved. And why this was such a roiling mess inside me was because love traveled right alongside the hate. I loved my father, clinging to my certainty that beneath the withholding bitterness of him coursed the blood of a real human being, a loving father. Hadn't I seen it after all?

And I loved the men who were following the only way they knew, the path their fathers had followed before them, their pain masked with bravado and humor. I loved them for their kindness to me. For their fear of the women they desperately needed to bolster their sense of themselves as good men. They gave the women a twisted kind of power, a power that came from insisting that the women deny their own strength—a power reinforced by a certain kind of subservience, a false dependency, so that after a while, it seemed to me, they had forgotten their strength.

Yet I loved the women, too. I saw the way they gathered when there was trouble, figured out how to make the paycheck work, had dreams and plans for their children. They took care of the sick and the dying. They faced death in a way the men did not.

And what of me?

I had done my father's work since remembering, and while I could no longer honor the making of trophies, I still loved the physicality of the work, the sense of being let into a mystery of what lay beneath flesh. I could not help loving the work I was apprenticed to do, as if an old familiar language of movement and gesture lay dormant until I put my hands to the fur.

But now that I had seen the mourning fox at the bone cage and been visited in the dream, I had to admit that for a long time the slight ripple in my own flesh each time I cut into theirs was telling me that the animals are intelligent and feeling beings, and how could I go on, knowing the truth of it.

Worn out by my questions and my walking, one late afternoon I threw myself down on the bank of the river, in despair, and there I rocked and cried.

"Uh huh. . . uh huh." Rhythmic and low. Beside me.

I feared this was yet another sign of my growing insanity and it took me a while to muster the courage to turn to see if indeed there was someone there behind me or empty confirmation of my deteriorating state. I slowly lifted my head from the cradle of my arms and saw that across the river stood Lou and the bear and fox watching me. *Oh no.* They were looking behind me and so I turned. It was an old woman. Putting her fishing gear down on the ground, then folding her skirt underneath her, she sat down beside me.

"Something is plowing you under good," she said.

Now what do I do, I thought, unable to think of a way to put her off the scent. We sat for some while. I stared at the fiddlehead ferns poking their heads up on the bank of the river, coiled and fuzzy.

"You're the taxidermist's daughter, aren't you," she said. "Don't be alarmed, old women make it their business to know who is who."

Silence.

"I'm Sophie Carson, a friend of Carl's, who comes into your father's shop."

I had heard of her. Carl liked her. The other men thought maybe she was a little crazy, but an excellent fisher.

"You okay, Louise?"

It wasn't lost on me that she called me Louise. I wanted to respond, but the words jammed in my mouth. I had such a resistance to speaking them as though there were only so many and they would be inadequate to this thing I was walking around trying to feel my way into. Or out of. I shrugged my shoulders, nodded my head, yes, trying to be casual to override my embarrassment at being so "plowed under."

The silence seemed easy in her company, and I was beginning to settle into my habitual quiet when she started getting to her feet. "Alright then," she said, "you just seemed so distressed that I just thought . . . Well, anyway, I've got some fish to fry up so I'll be on my way."

133

I panicked. "It's just that . . ."

She sat back down and turned to me. "What?"

"I'm lost." It was true. I felt as if I'd found the animals and yet lost my people, with no place on earth where I could be fully at home. Just walking.

"Go on," she said.

"I'm trying to figure something out. But when things start to clear, I end up back where I started."

Sophie laughed, "Reminds me of a coyote I was tracking once, for the fun of it. I realized I was walking in circles and that I'd been following the coyote following me! Right there all the time."

When I didn't laugh, she sat back down.

"I've come to believe that a question that eludes capture is usually a good thing," she said.

"What do you mean?"

"It means if it's not simple, you're probably onto something. A good question takes you places you might not choose to go."

We both sat and considered the truth of that, Sophie's blue eyes scanning the edge of the woods.

Did she see them, I wondered.

"The fox cried," I said. "Its heart was broken. No one ever told me."

"Maybe they don't remember."

I considered that. If she was right, it seemed a relief somehow, that they weren't cruel, they just did not remember.

"But it seems you do," she said.

"What do I remember?"

"That the animals are people."

I was stunned into a momentary silence to hear Sophie say what I had been thinking, and relieved, too.

All the stored-up words poured out in relief. "I've worked with my father since I can remember, it's what I know, the animals, their fur, their skins. There is something in it that I love, but," I started to shake then and gripping my knees tight to my chest, willed myself to be still. Sophie waited. "But now it seems cruel," I said. "I'm circling something, some dark truth, something isn't right about it, but then again, sometimes it seems like it's calling me, there is a kind of quiet there and it's almost as if everything is there, I mean *everything*. You know? And then they're all mixed together and I can't sort it out. . . ."

As she sat and listened to me, it seemed we were inside that everything now, the two of us, the river, the fiddleheads, the late afternoon sun, the pungent scent of wet earth. Some place out of time.

Sophie waited.

"But what I think is that they have honest-to-god lives that they care about."

"Yes," she said, "a different people with honest-to-god lives. My grandmother would include trees in that too, and plants."

"Did she kill them?"

"Yes."

"Did she take their skin?"

"Yes."

"How could she do that if they are people?"

"Well, she'd starve if she didn't. And freeze."

I considered that.

"It's an older understanding, Louise. She made offerings to the animals, she treated them with respect. Grandma knew who she was and who she was serving. She took from life and she owed life."

"How do you learn that?"

"Seems to me you are learning it."

We didn't speak much after that and sat for a good while. I remember the dappled light on Sophie's face, reflected through the young leaves and from the moving water and I wondered then if she was human or the old woman in the river. Maybe rivers were people, too. Maybe she lived in water and had materialized from it.

135

Anything seemed possible in light of what she was telling me, in my deepest need. She seemed older than old, her face filled with creases and their tributaries.

"What and who are you serving?" she asked.

I turned to her, "What do you mean?"

"I mean," she said, pulling back and looking at me, "What are you living for, Louise? If you figure that one out, life has a way of falling into place, even if it's more difficult." She grinned a wolfish grin at that, which put me on edge.

I wondered if maybe she *was* a bit crazy and I didn't know how to feel about that. If she was, she seemed to do okay, and if she wasn't, perhaps I wasn't either, but the rest of the world was.

She got to her feet, gathered up her fishing gear and, in parting, said, "My grandmother was one of the wisest people I knew. Sometimes it's the crazy ones who are on to something. It's been good talking to you, Louise. Carl knows where I live. Come any time."

I hated to see her go and I couldn't stand the tension a moment longer. She was unnerving, seeming to live in the strange world I had entered.

I got up and bolted toward home. When I got there, breathless and sweaty, the house was empty and I remembered that my parents were working late and it was my night to cook dinner for them. Restless still with everything that had happened, I put on my soft boots, grabbed some nuts from the pantry and headed out to the woods, desperate for clarity, to chew on Sophie's questions.

As I walked I made note of the disarmed traps waiting for fall and the winter fur. I had seen them many times, but this time I took out my pencil and pad and marked where they were. Someone in me had made a decision even while I pondered Sophie's question, someone who knew who and what she would serve.

I walked up a little knoll to sit under a large many-branched white pine, the wind making a kind of ocean music through the shiny needles while from deep in the body of the old tree came a mournful creaking song. Red squirrels scolded me, but soon quieted, forgot about me, and came down to crack open last year's cones, releasing seed that would become squirrel and tree, raccoon and deer. I thought about how the people would eat the seed-eating animals, marveling at how life travels through us and becomes us and we become other. This seemed to me a miracle, a continuous thread that I needed to hang onto.

It's an older understanding, Louise. She made offerings.

I fingered the seeds of the last few years trying to string them together into some kind of litany, a prayer for guidance, but to what god I did not know. It seemed life was trying to get something into me. I thought of Mary Estey killed for witching, accused of having the powers to bend fate, to walk invisible in the world, to heal, to harm. Was that an older way, now of the devil?

I imagined being that, doing that, walking invisible along the river, springing foot hold traps, freeing fox and raccoon, disarming beaver traps. But then I thought of those who, come fall, would need the animals to feed their families, and how if I used magic powers to free the animals, those people would suffer. There seemed no way out of this. Loving my people, both human and animal, seemed impossible. And besides, what magic powers did I have?

The air grew cooler and I stood to walk on home. I was shortcutting through witch hazel meadow when I saw her. A fawn, mostly concealed by mountain laurel, lay curled into a posture of waiting and trust. I sat a good distance from her, not wanting to alarm her mother should she return. As we gazed at each other, between us another world opened up, a world through which we could travel to each other, travel through air perhaps, not like the devil but like a blessing. I could smell the blood, the birth blood mingling with the smell of my own rust colored blood, the blood of the animals I had held in my hands, the blood of my own birth. Even the blood I had released from my father's hand.

Looking at the fawn, I remembered I was new like that once, made from the blood and flesh of my mother and everything that had fed her. I imagined crawling back into her body, being her fawn nestled in the bony bowl of her pelvis, under her heart, her thrumming blood. She was all mother then, my mother, animal mother, first mother, a loamy and fertile cradle.

Perhaps here was the source of what I was trying to remember, or what was trying to remember me, the root of the call to bone and pelt. Perhaps this primordial beginning, knowable only by a kind of memory that lives in the body, was the source of my longing. And my people's longing. That seemed true to me.

They don't remember.

And I had forgotten what I had remembered in the dream, looking into the eyes of the fox, and now it had come back to me. I am animal, too. We are kinned. How could we forget it. It must call to us out of our instinct, down the blood line.

My father rose before me then, and the men in the shop and their need to master their animal nature, their needs. Theirs was a fierce forgetting, a wanting to rise above the legacy of the truth. This being animal. A forgetting that destroyed the most tender human things in its war on life. Including their own hearts.

Relief and gratitude washed over me. All my questions and confusion had been keeping me busy stumbling around in the dark, while someone or something had been using the dark to teach me. Who or whatever that was, I decided I was serving that one.

The dream had haunted me, in sleeping and in waking, wanting something from me. And now I knew it was to receive the animal heart. To carry the burden of the knowledge that we are related. However I would proceed now must bear witness to the truth of that.

Oh, now I was really afraid. There was no turning away from what I knew and I would have to be as fierce in my remembering as they in their forgetting. I was no longer a child.

IT WAS NEARLY DARK when I came back to myself, startled by the snorting doe discovering me there, dangerously close to her fawn. She pawed the ground and moved toward me and I stood quickly and backed away. Seeing my retreat, she stilled, looking me in the eyes, curious, it seemed.

The frogs had started their chorus at Frog Pond and I followed their call through the darkened woods. They were guiding me back to the dirt road that would lead up the hill to home. When I approached the pond, they knew and went silent. And when I was some mysterious distance away they took up the song again, *spring, spring.* And I felt it too, like I'd been given a way to love my mother and my father and my people in their ignorance. A way to begin again, to proceed. But I was no fool, even then one so young, for I knew they fought for the way they thought it was and should be, stood by it, defended it as the way because it was the only thing they knew, this religion of severance.

Instead of going directly home, I returned to the shop, entering Salome's side, not my father's, and I sat on the turquoise sofa with its tufted and tasseled cushions, while my mother waited for me to explain what had brought me in her door without her having to ask for my help. She gave me a cup of tea.

"My name is Louise."

My words traveled a distance of some fourteen years, and they entered her, I could see, like a homecoming. She started to rise and come to me, but I put up my hand. She sat.

"You gave me to my father."

A flush rose on my mother's face. I continued. "It's not such a bad thing to be seen as a gift. It is a beautiful thing in a way. And you couldn't have any way of knowing that I wasn't yours to give. But I am telling you now. I am taking myself back from both of you. And I release you from any guilt you might carry about me."

I felt as though the words I spoke were Louise's words, that I was hearing them as freshly as my mother was hearing them. It is curious how another truer self can live in us without our

139

knowledge. She had been taking in the world in her own way apparently, ready to step forward when the time was right. I did not feel possessed by a stranger. I felt both surprised and yet familiar, as though she was a faint echo I had been straining to hear my whole life, like trees shaped by wind and light. I had been shaped by the pull of Louise's soul, that truest thing that could not be shattered by circumstance.

We sat in silence. There were daffodils on the table, a deep saturated yellow in the lamplight, in a gleaming crystal vase that had passed through many generations. The vase stood on a tablecloth the color of blue chicory, and I thought, how like my mother, and I could appreciate her eye for beauty. And I hoped that it had entered me, too. I told her that and she smiled.

While I made supper, slicing the white potatoes and strong onions, I replayed the conversation with my mother. I was proud and surprised about my declaration. I had taken myself back from both of them, and with sudden clarity knew that I would now offer myself to the animals, to my own soul.

When I returned to my father's shop the next day, I carried the memory of Sophie and the fawn and the deer inside me, the memory of what had seemed to rise up out of the land the day before. I didn't yet know how to proceed, knowing what I now understood. I sat, my hands in my lap, the skinning knife laying across my palm, its mother-of-pearl handle speaking of the sea, the curved blade gleaming praise of its maker. My father's voice startled me out of my reverie.

"There's work to do, Louise."

Not moving a muscle, I cut my eyes at him and he backed away.

I sat waiting for some way to come to me. Speaking to that one or many who had been teaching me in the dark, I prayed, *my name is Louise, please tell me what to do.* While I smoothed layers of paper onto the paper-mache mounts, I tried to strip layers off my mind, the sediment, the strata hundreds of years old that estranged

140

me from the world. I wanted to shuck off what separated me from cell, from story, from creation. I didn't want to use the world, I wanted to live in it. I wanted to be fully human.

I entered my own story of how it could be different. Why not? What is there to lose now? It could not be worse. Sophie told me her grandmother made offerings. What was my offering? What did I have that was precious that I could give as a way of trying to make it right between the animals and my people?

I WALKED AND THOUGHT about what I could offer that was of value. I asked the air and it came to me then. *What of all those words you have stored up inside?* My voice had been the thing that was mine, my silence the one thing I had shared in common with the dead. And that I now secretly shared with the trees and sparingly with my mother. If I spoke and how I spoke was one of the ways I had held onto myself all these years, and from that I knew that language has power. I decided I would offer my words to the animals, to their spirits. And I would listen.

It was all I had to give. I imagined that my listening to the stories their bodies told of their deaths, their last moments, would somehow repair the harm. I imagined that my words would reach into some place where things might be made right.

I wanted proof. I wanted their skins below my hands to jump and itch. I wanted the bones to vibrate. I wanted them to give me a sign that I was on the right path. I wanted the one who had been teaching me in the dark to speak. But I had to go on faith.

From that time on, I approached the animals as people. I took it upon myself to be the mediator between the killer and the killed. I would do what I could, in my unskilled way, to atone for wrongs. I would be grateful for what was taken.

While I still did not speak to my father, I took to mumbling over the skins when I worked, which irritated him and that pleased me, I admit. As I worked, I would apologize, *I'm sorry they don't remember how it should be.* Over time, I sensed the story of their death.

Perhaps they had decided to trust me. Perhaps this is why I was spared, why Lou was taken. I came to see that the hunter's heart enters in with arrow or bullet or shot. Enters in with the swing of the ax, the slice of the knife across the throat. I know that their whole intent, who they really are, is known by their prey who convey it to me. I saw it as my job to stitch the world back together.

I said prayers to restore the animals, *may your people prosper.*

I blessed those who hunted for food for their table. I asked the animal's mercy for their mistakes. I asked the animal spirit to be generous with those who hunted with heart and respect. That they have enough. And no more.

That is how it started, innocuous enough. But soon other words came as I skinned and fleshed and grained, as I stitched the skins along the back of the neck. I took up the powers of cursing as well as blessing.

There, I admit it. I stitched in the curse of knowledge. *Every time you look at me, know what you have done. May you wake up weeping.* I cursed the aim, envisioning bullets missing their targets, great white flags of tail escaping into the brush. I would demand reparations on behalf of the animal spirit. In working the pelts, I sometimes cursed the leghold traps to rust open, to break, to spring closed empty. I did everything for which my ancestor had been hung. It seemed a kind of justice to me, to use the store of imagined curses that had already been paid for with her life.

In my zealousness and my youth, I was arrogant and I missed the subtlety of things. I see that now. I moved from blessing and gratitude, from asking and offering, to cursing. I was young and it was difficult to hold the complexities in my mind. I was trying to make some kind of reparation. And there, too, was the magnetic pull of my own power. Yet, in my defense, when I encountered cruelty, when I felt it under my hands, animal as trophy, as swagger nailed to the wall, the den of motherless kits, the gut-shot deer dying a painful death, the rotting and skinless bear carcass, I cursed.

I was imagining a new world, a different way, or perhaps the old one Sophie spoke of. It helped me survive the way it was.

It frightened me when the men began to remark on the astonishing luck or skill visited on a particular one among them, and the equally astonishing degree of bad luck visited on another. That I was attempting to work with some power, of course, was clear to me. But I had as much doubt as any of my people would have that there was anything to it other than it was helping me to survive work that would have split my soul in two.

The women in my mother's shop began to speak about their men waking in the night weeping, grief pouring out of them, then turning to their wives tenderly. Something was happening, and while they were moved, they were alarmed at this change. I was, too, but I thought, better weeping than numb. Better to hunt with a weeping heart than a dead one.

I worried about what I might have set loose, alternately believing and dismissing—consequence or coincidence?

Even so, I carried on, wading deeper.

I walked by the river. Watching for leghold traps, I sprung them with sticks, stripped with my knife, marked by my teeth. I wondered if the one who set the trap would see those tiny bite marks while, cursing, he reset the traps, and again when I sprung that one, and that one and that one. It did not occur to me then to despair that there were too many traps and not enough Louises to spring them all.

I WAS SIXTEEN. I'd gotten careless I suppose, or been lucky till then. One day he loomed up before me on the path. I had always watched for Bud, knowing the danger he carried. He was a cold man who killed without remorse or regret and I could feel that. My mind swerved around the kindnesses he had shown me. His voice, quiet and tentative, "It's *you*, Lou?" turned menacing at what in his mind was betrayal. "*You* been fucking with my traps?"

And I said to him, my voice flat, "Lou is gone," and he looked just a little bit afraid then—who was I, a ghost? Crazy?

It was late fall, a bite in the air, the ground covered with leaves scuttling at our feet. I'd become unwary, springing his traps for two years now. I was fleetingly impressed by his patience. I knew the kind of hunter he was, and this perhaps was the most skill he'd ever shown, waiting me out, biding his time. If I had been a deer, I'd be dead. He was betrayed by Lou, yet who was this standing before him now, with the flat, unafraid voice?

I would not show fear and, as I knew it would, this angered him. And he came for me, excited and challenged by my fearlessness. I was prey now—would he bite into my heart the way they did once, taking in the vitals of the ones they killed? He pinned me under him, his breath raspy and strong, the moving river, the last of the leaves floating down around us. The fall-blue sky did not descend to my defense, nor the river rushing past, nor deer or fox over whose kin I had prayed. The trees sheltered the act, as they had sheltered so many bloody goings on. Witness, again and again, to the unraveling of the human world, the broken treaties. How life could still grow among such violations was a mystery, but life makes life and would continue. And I would continue, too.

He was a big man, Bud was. Every ounce of him enlisted in the project of controlling the world, red faced, flushed, an angry red mountain of a man who wanted to eat my heart, who, when he had, would still be hungry, more hungry, starving. He split me then. There is more than one kind of knife. He split open the husk of me and arced above me, this mountain, pinning me beneath the weight of centuries, of need, of want, of right.

"This'll do it. This'll do it," he kept muttering while I bounded, white tail flagging over the river, to stand and witness from the other side, Louise splitting open, taken like so many before her. He split open the husk of me and planted himself there, his seed, but *my* earth. I would not receive the bitterness of it, the rage of it. Never. It would not become a bitter harvest, no matter how that seed took and planted itself, I would not sell my soul in that way. The harvest would be mine. What looked like submission was not.

There was a litany in my mind, *never, never, never*. And so a part of me waited across the river for it to be done, and I saw up in the sky a large and flapping raven, descending, looking for the way into the angry red mountain, into its heart. Or was I the raven? I saw it inside my mind, and outside too, a confusion of wings everywhere, the descending black presence and Bud over me, eyes squeezed shut, ramming into me, "This'll do it," the black wings headed straight for him and I screamed his name in warning, the wings and claws covering him, us, me screaming over and over, "Bud! Bud!" his eyes flying open then, confused and alarmed at finding me beneath him, at tearing me open.

And then the raven struck. Bud seemed to convulse, his face a contortion of pain and pleasure and then a softening, a kind of recognition, almost a smile, and he said, "Mother, oh, mother, forgive me . . . " And then I lay under the mountain and I waited as hesitantly, carefully the deer returned, the raven perched on the bulk of the man that crushed me. Waiting to see.

Warmth ran from me and I burned, and leaves fell with a soft clatter against those already fallen, making new earth. I closed my eyes, I don't know how long. Then there was the river, the sky, no raven, no deer, but Louise here pinned beneath centuries of need, of want, of starving. Louise taken, but not possessed.

I waited for him to move, to make a sound, who would he be now? The old Bud?

I lay there under him, the pieces of me slowly coming home to me, Louise. I realized then that he was dead. His ravaged and dead heart was truly dead. A horror swept through me at the lifeless weight of him and I thought of all the deer and fox and bear and others, the dead weight of them taken by Bud. Taken but never received. I lifted his lifeless arm flung down beside me and rolled out from under him. I sat beside him watching him. I was shaking, my whole self wracked with shuddering. And then I cried, for myself, for the animals. Even for Bud.

It took all my strength to roll over his dead weight and look into his face. I had to be sure. Then I left him there, his pants down around his thighs, his bulk left for discovery, perhaps by fox, racoon, fisher, certainly bacteria. Now he would pay his debt to what and whom he had taken from. It seemed fair to me.

I went to the river and I scooped water up to wash myself, swollen and hurting. And as I chanted in my head, *my earth, my earth,* I swore I would not let him eat me from the grave. I would not allow this violation to grow, to fester. What was done was done and I would be Louise.

SOPHIE WAS THE ONE I went to. I walked the miles to her house and I told her Bud was dead and what he had done. She took me in and cleaned me up and sent word to Carl to let my parents know that I was staying with her for a couple of days. Salome and John were so cautious about me by then, so skittery in my company, they did not question it. Sophie helped me with some old ways taught to her by her grandmother. She mixed up a wash to flush Bud out of me, to heal my split flesh.

The next day we talked. I told her everything, what I had been doing, springing the traps, cursing and blessing. I told her the thought that had moved through my mind, lying under Bud, that whatever had been planted in me would be mine. Not his, mine.

She agreed that there are all kinds of seeds, that it was up to me to grow that harvest in such a way that it would yield life. But she looked at me with worry, I saw that.

I was worried, too, that the invisible thing that Bud carried had entered me and lodged there. That it would grow into my own bitterness and fear. That what he had really hoped to do, to violate my soul, had happened and could not be undone. I told this to Sophie.

146

She took my hands in hers. "Louise, you can't erase the brutality, but you don't let him take what's still yours to give. Your wholeness. Your soul. Remember this, Louise, because forgetting it will be the death of you. Understand? It's in the forgetting that the violence can do its work."

Yet I felt robbed, too, of a satisfying and immediate vengeance that I fantasized would give me power. I told myself that if he had not died, I would have stalked and killed him.

I see now that I was saved from that bitter pursuit by an unseen hand. By raven? By his desiccated and clogged heart swollen with bitter want? Life takes care of life, somehow.

She put her hands on me then, like her grandmother would, she said, pulling out the poison of Bud, those demons of undoing that might have entered me.

"Vengeance would not help a thing, Louise," she said as she brushed me with smoke and with feathers. Together we burned my clothing and I wrapped myself in a blanket and slept for two days.

I dreamed of a immense and angry red mountain arcing over me at the center of which was my red heart, the one the fox had returned to Lou, the one Bud had split open, the one he had eaten, becoming the red heart of the deer, all the animals taken, our hearts split open like a husk, like the heart of me had been split open and I saw the seed planting itself inside of me, bloody and luminous.

I left Sophie and returned home. Night after night I dreamed. Day after day I walked. I worried the dream—what and who was the luminous seed? Was I pregnant? No. Sophie had seen to that.

This is what happens, I thought, to those who dare to challenge the centuries, who challenge the taking, the violation, the terror. But I would not agree to forget. I would remember. Bud had made real the magnetic power of longing, the danger of emptiness and the lengths to which we would go to fill it.

Now I knew that there were consequences, like my ancestor before me, perhaps. The invisible thing we opposed, she, the devil, me, the violation, that would have us betray our soul, rose up and

147

fought back, leaving its mark on our bodies. My body. Whether it won would be up to me. I had decided that he would not leave the kind of scar that would seal me from my own heart. I would go on. After all, had not the animals done so? It did not escape me that I was hard to kill, and I was pleased about that. Was that the legacy of my long dead grandmother?

Bud was found by hunters. I heard the men whispering the story at the shop. Not wanting to offend me, they spoke in low voices, gathering ranks around the details, protecting the dead man's reputation. The women weren't so delicate as they passed each detail among them, questioning, outraged and yet not surprised. Roxie said she knew he would end up dead with his pants around his feet some day. Even she, though, had to wonder what he was doing out there on the path by the river getting himself off. And I wondered about his murmured "mother, oh mother," his plea for forgiveness. Was his mother there to receive him even in such disgrace? Is that how it works? I learned that he had not been found before a few meals were made of his flesh and I was glad of it.

I never told Salome and John about what had happened. I feared they would blame me because I had provoked Bud by messing with his traps. It was common knowledge that someone had done so, but who was a mystery.

The fall deepened into winter and I walked, thinking what to do with my life. How to make sense of all that had happened.

One day as I walked along the river path I came to the spot where Bud had overtaken me. I had avoided it until then. It was winter now, the leaves all gone, the ground was covered in snow, a pristine blanket laid over all that had happened there on that day when the raven seized Bud's heart.

The slender white birches leaned in still, leafless against the blue sky, silent. Chickadees and nuthatches gossiped about me and flitted from branch to branch. There was evidence of a rabbit and fox encounter in the thickets by the river, fresh bloody tracks trotting off to den telling me who had won that old agreement. There was no sign of another taking just one season past.

The land witnesses and absorbs our crimes against each other, I thought, and wondered what stories it tells after we are gone. Or did it even happen?

I tamped a space for myself and sat down there, quieting myself, forcing myself to remember his body humped over me, his body eaten on by mice and fox. Would the river tell that story? In the murmur of water I again heard the echo of *this'll do it, this'll do it.*

I laid down then where Bud had died, where the last of the child in me had died, and imagined my body a feast for fox and mouse and fisher. How rarely our bodies give back what we so freely take from the other animals, how rarely our deaths wear the face of tooth and claw.

I had walked along the river for years now. I walked the deer path, I tracked the fox, the migration of hawks and now I traced the path of the terrible need that had driven Bud, in the end, to rape me. I sensed this need too in myself, this terrible need to be near the animals, even their fur and bones, taken in an unholy way, that aroused a longing in me. But for what? Whom?

Everything is alive, Sophie told me that. Every animal, every tree, every dream. And, I thought, if something is alive, it has hunger doesn't it? And if everything is alive, then longing is alive, too, and maybe it is hungry.

I considered this, lying on the snowy ground warmed by the winter sun, looking up at the sky, the same sky that the raven had descended from on that day. *This'll do it, this'll do it.* Do what? I felt its urgency and I knew that Bud had seized me, desperate to kill an insatiable hunger once and for all. Hunger and longing whispered a tale of weakness in Bud's ear, while seizing told a hero's story. He had done me a terrible wrong, yet he was only one more actor in the story of terrible wrongs committed to extinguish invisible gnawing hungers.

Hungry for what? What does longing eat? I knew that longing is what pulled me into the woods and onto the path. It took me, seized me, and brought me into that world, which seemed to soothe the gnawing until the next time it seized me.

I listened to a red-tailed hawk calling overhead, her particular piercing cry of longing. I wished then that she longed for me as I yearned for her. I lay there looking up into a winter blue sky, the hawk sailing invisible vectors. I sent my yearning into the air and I imagined the hawk filling the air, too, with her yearning. The air between us seemed to swell with a nearly unbearable sweetness and grief that cut to the center of me.

I wanted to jump up and run, to find a way out of this terrible pain. I wanted the hawk to live forever and I knew he wouldn't but I wanted him to, and for our stories to live side by side in this terrible yet sweet unnamed thing always. Because in this unbearable feeling, I felt more Louise than I ever had. Not alone. And I found myself wanting to possess this moment, not to have to face its ending, leaving me bereft and alone again.

I lay there and thought about this, how I wanted to grasp the moment, never have to let it go so that I would never be lonely and hungry again. But that is not possible. Could that be it? Might this hunger that draws us out of ourselves, that makes us reach beyond ourselves, so often with violence and grasping, as Bud had seized me, might this hunger be for that sweet thing that sometimes happens between us and the other? The thing that issues from neither of us but from what is born between us, a mysterious something that no one can own, much as we try. What I sought in my possession of bone and fur. What the men sought in their trophies.

I lay there a long time, sending my longing into the sky. It was like a riddle, what does one feed longing? I could not possess this sweetness, I could not possess this hawk, I could only meet it in the space between, opened by longing. Or I could seal myself off from ever enduring such piercing again. Like my father in his isolated world.

What does longing eat?

Your willingness to bear it.

Is this the harvest?

It is.

Elation and a sorrow filled me.

Bear it.

I got up then and walked on. Who lives that way? No one I knew except for Sophie. Not my father, nor my mother, nor the people who came to the shops. How could one, in finding the way out of loneliness and the torture of possession, walk such a solitary path?

Choose.

I walked. The sky had clouded over and I had not noticed. Snow began to fall, light snow, big fat unhurried flakes fell, coating my hair, lying clean upon the old snow. I stuck out my tongue, cold dissolving and refreshing in my mouth.

Could I give it back, the harvest, could I refuse it, I wondered. Could I forget? This harvest is too heavy to bear, too sorrowful to carry. Did I have to endure a life bereft of human community? It didn't make sense. But it was how it was. I could see that.

I came upon the body of a deer in the snow. She lay at the base of a white oak, her body split down the middle, open and emptied, her eyes milky with death. Tracks led to and from her body, a raven sat in a nearby tree, watching me.

The snow fell around us and I entered the dream of her, the cave of her body, an altar open to the sky in the white snow. I kneeled down at this altar, this deer, this one who isn't remembered as one, as a being, this one who feeds all who come, fox, eagle, even the demanding and rude raven, even me, Louise, who had been taken and whose people had been taking, taking for so long.

It was like being lost in the forest and coming upon another red mountain, but unlike the angry red mountain of Bud, this mountain had entry, its red and luminous cave opening into the heart, the language of snow falling down on us like a benediction.

Choose.

This deer knew who she was, brought down by someone who did not know who she was, or he was, a hungry ghost. She knew that she was deer, and plant, tree and wind, and snow beds. She was herd, and milk, and rut, and now food. Now bird and fox, now bacteria. Now Louise.

I lay down then, inside the cradle of her broken ribs open to the sky like a boney hand. Offering. Beseeching. And I thought, this is how it's done. I will eat the heart of all of it, and lay in her cradle and wait for the new one to be planted in my heart, for the new one to be birthed, no longer a child, but a woman now.

Lou was gone, the taxidermist's daughter gone. I had been split open by the fleshy knife, been split like the bloody deer's body, my heart had been eaten like the deer's heart had been eaten, but I would suck the vitality from that act, the split husk of me making new life, new ground to stand on, for the one who is here now. The luminous red seed. Me. Louise.

No longer the taker, I am the one who receives and gives, who meets the other in the mutual space of longing. I will walk out of here, out of her bloody womb a new woman. This is how I will cross over using everything that has happened, every bone, every muscle, every sinew, every tooth, every wound, every beauty. Every bit of what I have harvested. Of what has been given to me.

Afraid, I lay in the deer's body, waiting, the snow coating my hair, my eyelashes. The raven perched on the fracture of ribs watching me, the one I had become. I trembled with the cold, with the terror of the way that lay before me. Did I have the courage?

The raven laughed at me then.

And I knew.

I rose and walked away from the deer. I walked away as the one who had become someone else—the deer, the space between us, Louise. I walked back the way I had come.

In Gratitude

Thank you, tusen tak, tapa leigb, to the ineffable source of story who makes writing a kind of homecoming. To my dead and to my Ancestors, deep gratitude for this life I've been given.

Gratitude to Allan Johnson, my writer-scholar life partner, who has the soul of a poet and the mind of a scholar, who always amazes me in his willingness to read my work again and again. Who, with his faith in my writing, has helped to heal some of those inevitable wounds to my creative spirit. For our thirty-year navigation through life together.

To Anne Batterson, a true coyote spirit, for the adventurous courage she brings to the writing life and lends to me in times of doubt. For our many climbs up Hoar Mountain, deep conversations, and our shared passion to track the elusive coyote.

To Chivas Sandage and her Collinsville Writing Group for writerly companionship, consultation and inspiration while writing "The Taxidermist's Daughter."

To Deena Metzger, coyote pack member, *awhoooo,* teacher, Elder and deep Soul friend, for her wisdom and the courage to *always* follow the story, the dream, the call of Spirit no matter how early you have to get up, how late you get to bed, or how many detours it takes. For our many explorations, deep dives, and pee-in-our-pants laughter.

To Patricia Reis, who has walked beside me for many years now, diving into the deeps, dreams, disappointments and uncanny experiences finding names for the unnameable in deep support of the tribe of the Medial Woman.

Nora L. Jamieson lives in northwestern Connecticut where she writes, counsels women, and unsuccessfully tracks coyote. She lives with her spouse, Allan G. Johnson, their soulful dog, Roxie, and the sorrowful and joyful memory of four beloved goats and three dogs.

Visit her website at www.norajamieson.com.

CPSIA information can be obtained
at www.ICGtesting.com
Printed in the USA
LVOW12s2040130616

492393LV00002B/477/P